Wall of Secrets

Prequel to the Vital Secrets Series

D.F. Hart

The Vital Secrets Series

Visit *2ofharts.com* to sign up for my newsletter and get a special bonus supplement to the series!
Follow me on:
BookBub
Facebook

Goodreads

COPYRIGHT

Acknowledgements

I would very much like to say a heartfelt "Thank you" to:

My husband Rick, who for a time becomes a 'writing widower' when I get rolling.

My family and friends, who patiently and with enthusiasm endure more than one round of "hey, read this for me and tell me what you honestly think".

Lastly, to friend and fellow author A.W. Exley, who spoke truth to me and encouraged me to follow my dreams.

I could not have done this without your support.

Foreword

"Those who do not remember the past are condemned to repeat it." -George Santayana

With Hitler's defeat in 1945 came a Germany divided into four sections, each occupied in turn by the British, the French, the Americas, and the Soviets. This had been decided upon by the inter-Allied European Advisory Committee. Berlin itself was at first divided into three zones; later a fourth was carved out for the French. The Soviets arrived first in Germany's capital and used various tactics to stall the other Allied powers from reaching their agreed-upon zones. The other Allied nations were finally granted access to their zones of Berlin around eight weeks after the war had ended.

The American, British, and French zones began the daunting task of restoring day-to-day life activities to the people of Germany in their sections. The Soviet zone was equally as energetic about reviving a political system with a decidedly Communist bent in its sector. Enter Walter Ulbricht, a native German firmly entrenched in Communist thinking. To quote Frederick Taylor's "The Berlin Wall" – "It was clear from the first day that Ulbricht and his band were tools of the occupiers" (Taylor, 2006, Pg. 41). Ulbricht, as Stalin's mouthpiece in Germany, presented many challenges to the Allied powers; in this author's opinion these challenges were blatant attempts to get the Allied powers to leave Germany. Among the more famous incidents is the "Berlin Blockade", which lasted from June the twenty-fourth 1948 until May the twelfth 1949. The Soviet-controlled zone attempted to halt any supplies coming in to West Berliners. This missive was unsuccessful, as Americans and Brits took to the skies to deliver much-needed rations, with the help of use of airfields in the French sector. This action was later dubbed the "Berlin Airlift".

In the first twelve years, 1945 to 1957, the Soviet zone lost approximately one-sixth of its population to the West. The main reasons for this were, quite simply, a better, less restrictive standard of living and a new currency, the Deutschmark (D-mark), which was not undervalued like the Reichsmark still being used in East Germany. On the twenty-sixth of May 1952 East Germany erected a literal border around its entire territory – except its section of Berlin. Berlin remained open and relatively passable between the four zones. There were checkpoints, to be sure, but freedom of movement still occurred, as evidenced by the approximately 60,000 East Berliners who commuted to the West each day to work.

In 1953 Ulbricht asked yet again for permission to finish 'securing' East Germany by closing off the Soviet section of Berlin from the rest of the city. Stalin gave the green light for this, but before any plan could be enacted to make the Berlin border a reality, Stalin suffered a massive stroke and died on March fifth. His successor, Nikita Khrushchev, halted the plan to extend a physical barrier through Berlin itself.

By mid-1961, however, the hemorrhage of population from East over into West had reached dangerous levels. Ulbricht and his Soviet masters agreed something had to be done. The plan, codenamed 'Rose', was dispatched with precision and was completed within twenty-four hours. On Sunday August 13, 1961, the first in what would become a series of obstacles was placed to cut off East Berlin from West Berlin – approximately ninety-six miles of razor-topped barbed wire. An additional, more solid structure comprised of concrete was erected in 1962, about one hundred yards away from the original fence. By 1975 the 'Wall' would actually be comprised of three separate stand-alone concrete structures; a devil's playground of mines, razor wire, and other booby traps situated between the walls and alternately referred to as 'no-man's land' or the 'kill zone'; in addition to armed guards and light towers.

As it was intended to, the Wall restricted travel. It also literally ripped families apart. As shown in the 1962 documentary "The Wall", East Berliners daring to even wave at their loved ones over in the West could be severely punished or killed. Some East Berliners living in taller buildings in proximity to the Wall jumped from upper-story windows to reach the West. Shortly afterward, the East German authorities had any west-facing windows in these buildings bricked up, and razor wire installed along the rooftops. Those seeking to leave East Berlin for West Berlin had three equally dangerous choices – 'run the gauntlet' of walls, wires, mines, and armed guards; tunnel underneath all the madness and hope to come up in a Western zone; or, as two families successfully did, find the means to literally fly over the Wall structures. Between its inception on that fateful day in 1961, and its demolition in 1989, some 170 people perished trying to reach freedom in the West.

Historical Data in Foreword retrieved from:
De Hoog, Walter. 1962. *The Wall*. Video
Documentary.
Taylor, Frederick. 2006. The Berlin Wall: A World
Divided, 1961 – 1989. Harper Collins.

Author's Note:

As a college freshman, I watched, along with the rest of the world, the extraordinary events taking place in November 1989 in Berlin. I suppose like many of my generation, while I understood that the Wall coming down was significant, I really didn't grasp the full impact of what the Wall being built in the first place had really meant. As I have aged (hopefully gracefully!), I have now come to understand that the Wall was a very real symbol of oppression and of dominance, a huge flash point in the onset of the Cold War, a demarcation not only of geography and territory but also of communism versus democracy.

But I asked myself – What if someone who wanted the Nazi movement to resurge had placed vital documents into the Wall for safekeeping? What if that someone retrieved those documents when the Wall fell, and set their plan in motion? **What if**?

And now, dear reader, please join me in exploring one possible answer to those questions.

D.F. Hart

SECTION ONE: Berlin – 1961 - 1962

MITTE DISTRICT, EAST BERLIN

CHAPTER ONE

It was the twelfth of April 1961, almost noon, and Manfred Amsel was a deeply worried man. He paced back and forth, back and forth, across the worn linoleum of the waiting room. His wife, Rose, was in labor a full two weeks early. Prayer after silent prayer went up as naturally as breathing. He ran his hands yet again through his hair, fumbled for yet another cigarette almost as an afterthought. Every fiber of his being willed his wife and child to be all right somewhere behind closed doors.

After what seemed an eternity, the doctor appeared, tired but smiling. "They're both just fine," Dr. Strauss said, laying a kind hand on Manfred's shoulder. "You'll be able to see them within the hour. I shall want to keep them for a few days, just to be sure. After that, you can take your little family home."

The doctor then walked away to a well-earned cup of coffee and a cigarette of his own.

Through his tears of joy, Manfred managed to light his cigarette, albeit with a shaky hand. He walked out into the sunshine, smiling and crying, a proud new papa. Life was complete.

Manfred had been the cause for his father's same happy tears in 1920's Berlin. His father, a mathematical genius, had sobbed with joy at his son's arrival on that cold winter day. An only child, Manfred's parents doted on him constantly, took him everywhere, and exposed him to the arts as much as possible. He was reading newspapers aloud to his father over breakfast by the time he was four, and by the age of nine, he firmly announced his intention to be a professor of world literature at Berlin University. Hitler's ascension to power, first as Chancellor in 1933, then as President in 1934, put an end to that plan.

Manfred's parents, outspoken intellectuals who did not agree with or wish to conform to Nazi ideals, were worried both for themselves and for their only son. Mother, perfectly balanced between sentiment and practicality, wanted to pack up the entire house but realized it was not possible. Some cherished things would have to stay behind. She woefully confined her efforts to clothes, family pictures, and a few mementos that could be easily fit into the suitcases. Taking a last look at what amounted to years of memories, she whispered a prayer of protection for her family and the house as they locked the front door, possibly never to return. In this manner in mid-1934, the Amsels left their beloved homeland and their small but cozy home, heading first for Amsterdam.

For all the stress of the preparation to leave, the trip itself was uneventful, a welcome surprise. They traveled to and through Amsterdam with no trouble at all, and booked passage on a steamer to England, safely out of harm's way.

Or so they thought.

They continued much as they had been – mother as a housewife and highly talented painter, father as a mathematics professor. Manfred continued to receive outstanding marks in school, despite the move, and was accepted into the University of Oxford on scholarship in 1937. Manfred used the time and opportunity well and attained a Master's in World Literature in 1941 at the age of twenty-one. He also proved proficient in languages, adding fluent English, French, and Russian to his native German. These would later prove to be more valuable than the degree.

In addition to his academic prowess, however, Manfred also possessed a kind and gentle heart, and an unwavering sense of right and wrong. It angered him to the core to hear reports of what Hitler's Germany was up to, and he grieved heavily for his homeland, in the arms of a madman, ripped asunder. He vowed privately to someday return to Berlin and do whatever he could to help restore Germany to a peaceful and harmonious nation. After his parents were killed in the Luftwaffe bombing blitz of London in September 1940, he had also vowed to do whatever it took to wipe the filth of Nazism off the face of the earth forever. This line of thinking led him quite naturally into the British intelligence community, who put him to good use as he could fluently speak, read, and write four languages, including that of the enemy. He individually pursued a doctorate in World Literature when he was not busy providing translation services for the Allied effort.

This entrance into the war effort also landed him what would become a lifelong friend. He met Max Jones quite by accident one day in February 1945 as he was heading to a routine briefing with his superior, Michael Smythe. The subject matter, as usual, was to discuss the results of his day's translation of intercepted German messages. When he arrived at Michael's office, he found one of the guest chairs already occupied. The stranger that rose from it and extended his hand in greeting turned out to be a young American Army intelligence officer who was assigned to a joint task force composed of Brits and Americans. Brown-haired, suntanned, with an easy grin and piercing green eyes, Max Jones had a laid-back Texas personality that Manfred immediately took to.

Michael explained that the task force needed not only a top-notch translator, but someone who would be willing to return to Berlin 'once this bloody war ends' and be the eyes-and-ears on the ground there, as it were. They informed Manfred that the inter-Allied European Advisory Committee had decided in 1944 that once Germany was defeated, it was to be divided into four zones of control – Soviet, French, Britain, and American. Max went on to say that if certain things went the way the Allies hoped, Berlin would fall before the year's end – but there was a bit of concern that if the Soviets arrived in Berlin first, they might make life difficult for the other Allied powers.

So, the task force needed someone, a native German with impeccable credentials, someone who could set up shop in the Soviet zone without attracting attention. This individual would be depended upon to pass information from the Soviet zone to the American and British zones if needed. Max and Michael believed Manfred was ideal because he also spoke French, English, and Russian. Would he do it?

Without hesitation, Manfred agreed. With one condition. "I have no training whatsoever, gentlemen. If you will remedy that so I can properly defend myself if necessary, you have a deal," Manfred stated solemnly.

Max grinned and replied, "Absolutely, Professor. I'll have you shooting through the ace of spades at fifty paces."

And so, Manfred went through an abbreviated version of combat training and 'spy school' condensed into one program. Although not detailed enough to render him a walking lethal weapon – Manfred was willing but there was not enough time – the training did involve firearms and self-defense, in addition to comprehensive instruction in sending and receiving coded messages, dead drops, and other crucial data he would be much more likely to use. Manfred once again proved a top student, including attaining marksman status on the pistol range. The Professor was now loaded for bear should the worst occur.

Manfred Amsel began the journey home to Berlin in early 1946, both as a professor and, if all went well, as an inside source within the Soviet sector for the British and Americans. He stopped in the American sector of Berlin to touch base with Max Jones for last-minute instructions, and to set up some basic drop schedules for routine messages. A radio transmitter and a weapon would be passed to him when it could be done safely, a piece at a time if necessary.

Upon his return to the Mitte district of the Soviet sector, he found his family's little home on Wilheim-Pieck largely unscathed, a sentiment that could not be echoed through much of the rest of Berlin. Fate seemed to have held the house of his childhood ready for his homecoming. There was one patch of roof that needed mending and the garden beds along the front were horrendously overgrown. The entire house smelled of dust and age and was badly in need of a thorough cleaning and painting, but overall, he counted himself lucky. So many other buildings were at least partially destroyed. Four lots down, two other houses had been blown away. A blackened crater full of debris was the only evidence they had existed.

He found the interior only in minor disarray; it had evidently been used to billet soldiers at some point before the Soviets housed their forces in larger accommodations. Crude bunk beds had been installed in the tiny loft bedroom where he used to sleep. He guessed the time and trouble to retrieve them was not worth the effort because they were still in place. In the living area and bedroom downstairs, some of the family furniture had been stacked against one wall to enable still more bunk beds to be put into service, judging from the marks on the floor. The rest of the furniture, he assumed, must now grace some Soviet officer's quarters.

Quietly settling in, he did his best to keep out of the way but to listen and observe as much as he could. No one in the Soviet sector knew he could speak, read, and write Russian. As a result, he could be sitting in the café, reading his paper, pretending not to notice as two young occupying soldiers at the next table talked in their native tongue. Manfred understood every word they said, although he gave no sign. Eavesdropping, while pretending not to, turned out to be extremely useful. On June eighteenth, 1948, he communicated to his friends in the American sector using a dead drop. He relayed information he'd heard about a blockade intended to cut off West Berlin's inbound supply routes. The only thing Manfred did not overhear was when it would start, but from the conversation he felt it was likely imminent. What later became known as the 'Berlin Blockade' began on June twenty-fourth.

He found that Humboldt University had reopened its doors, went and spoke to the chancellors, and was immediately taken on as one of its professors. The lifetime goal of teaching in Berlin had been achieved, although not in the way Manfred had dreamt it. In 1947, the University began to experience inner turmoil. The division ensued due to roughly half of the faculty and students being resistant to the Communist tone the University was espousing. Consequently, Freie Universität of Berlin was founded in December 1948 in the American Zone. Attaining teaching positions with each college would give Manfred the excuse he needed to be able to travel much more freely, but it had to look like it was beneficial to Communism or it would not be allowed.

As he had been teaching there for about two years, he felt bold enough to approach Humboldt's chancellors and humbly ask permission to teach both there and at the new university in the West. He needed to convince them that cooperation between the two universities could not only enhance Communist teachings in the East but persuade some individuals to return from the West. "One cannot proclaim Communist superiority without first drawing examples from the decadent West," he exclaimed. To his surprise, his bosses and their Soviet handlers agreed.

Permission was granted.

He uttered those words at great personal cost. Manfred fervently embraced the idea of democracy with all his heart. But for his personal safety, to maintain the ability to teach young minds in East Germany about other points of view, and to be able to continue to pass information westward, he had to pretend to cling to Communist beliefs. His parents did not raise a fool, so Manfred also became an 'intellectual' spy within academia. But his public stance enabled him to travel more freely among the Zones and, more importantly, generate and maintain valuable contacts in the American and British sections of the city.

Thanks to new Freie Universität credentials, the Soviet border guards no longer looked at him so closely – he became a regular fixture to and from through both Checkpoint Charlie at the American border and at Tiergarten, the beginning of the British zone. Every third or fourth trip he carried back into Soviet territory one piece of what would become his wireless radio transmitter. By the end of 1949, he had a fully functional independent means of contact to be used for emergencies only. By the end of 1950 he also was in possession of a Walther .380 and one-hundred rounds, also for emergencies only.

1952 saw the Soviets border off their entire section of Germany from the West – with the exception of the Soviet zone of Berlin. The Soviets thought they had caught the West unaware with this move. The Americans and Brits had in fact known about it roughly a week before it happened – thanks to Manfred, and two unwitting accomplices in the form of lower-level Russian soldiers complaining about their weekend passes being cancelled.

In early June 1954, on a brilliantly sunny afternoon, Manfred crossed into the American zone and was making his way toward Freie Universität to introduce his junior-level students to the works of Tolstoy. As he walked along, he was looking down at his notes for the day's lecture. Preoccupied, he walked straight into the person that would complete his world. Rose Meyer was an ethereal beauty, a petite twenty-four-year old brunette, with cornflower blue eyes that captured his heart the moment he looked into them. It was love at first sight. In that moment, he knew she was his future. He met and was immediately approved of by her parents, courted her passionately, and proposed on their seventh date. With an angelic smile, she accepted.

The Meyers had relocated to the West right after Berlin fell. They understood the forces at work politically, and that Manfred's public stance was not his true heart, but necessary to maintain. Manfred and Rose's father Klaus had many private discussions about the marked differences in East and West Berlin. Klaus was amazed that East Berlin itself had not yet been hidden behind a barrier as the rest of the Soviet zone had been in 1952. He cautioned Manfred to be vigilant in his dual role, but also to be ready when the time came to abandon the pretense and come to the West permanently.

June fourth, 1955, saw the happy couple married in the old and very beautiful Church of Reconciliation on Bernaur Strasse. It was the first and last time that Klaus and Emilie Meyer set foot in the Soviet zone since they left it ten years earlier. Rose, as beautiful as she already was, simply took Manfred's breath away when she walked down the aisle on her proud father's arm, dressed in her mother's wedding gown. As they stood together, reciting their wedding vows before God and their family, they made a perfect couple – she was small and slender, with dark hair enhanced by her white gown, and blue eyes radiant with happiness; he was tall and lanky, salt-and-pepper beginning at the temples of wavy, black hair, and piercing chocolate-brown eyes wet with emotion as he took this woman to be his wife.

After some thought, Klaus agreed that for Manfred to keep up appearances as a happy Communist, it would be necessary for Manfred and Rose to reside in the Soviet sector after the wedding. Manfred and his new bride returned to his family home in the Mitte district, on Wilheim-Pieck not far from the Church where they had been married, settling into life as newlyweds. The next five years were mostly uneventful for the couple, to their secret relief. The Stasi, East Germany's police, were rumored to move swiftly against anyone who opposed

Communist views. But Manfred's careful posturing over the last several years rendered him above suspicion.

Occasionally, Rose would accompany her husband on trips into the American sector and visit with her family while Manfred was teaching classes. During one visit in late September, 1960, Rose and Manfred announced to her family that their first child was on the way, due sometime around the first of May. Rose's parents erupted with joy. Klaus beamed as never before at the news he would become a grandfather, but he also worried deeply for his only daughter and son-in-law, whom he loved as his own. He reiterated to Manfred the need to have a plan in place to permanently escape to the West 'should the worst happen'. Neither man had any idea at the time how prophetic his stance would be.

Manfred awoke at two a.m. on April twelfth, 1961, to the sound of Rose moaning. Sitting upright in bed, he discerned through eyes still filled with sleep that his wife was standing in the doorway between the bath and bedroom. She was leaning against the doorjamb, attempting to call for him as contraction after contraction coursed through her petite but very pregnant body. After a few precious seconds ticked by, his brain registered what was happening. All six feet of him leapt from the bed to his wife in one bound, with surprising agility and grace. As the contraction subsided, Rose raised her beautiful, lightly sweat-glistened face to him and whispered with a little smile, "I think we ought to go now."

Even if the hospital were across town rather than a few blocks away, Manfred would still have gotten Rose there in the speed of light. He drove as fast as he dared to with such precious cargo. When they finally reached the front entrance, he abandoned all protocol and parked directly at the curb. In truth, it had only been about ten minutes since he'd gingerly helped his wife to the car at their home, but it felt like a lifetime. He helped Rose out of the car just as another contraction was beginning.

Manfred picked her up and, carrying her as he would a china doll, carefully made his way up the steps to the nurse's station just inside the doors. One look told the two nurses sitting there all they needed to know. A wheelchair was procured, and away went Rose with another brisk but capable nurse to parts unknown.

Manfred had only vaguely been aware of hearing Dr. Strauss' name being paged over the loudspeaker. *That means the doctor is on duty tonight, thank God*, he thought. *No waiting for the man to arrive.*

He turned to the nurses, who had been eyeing him with some amusement, and asked, "What do I do now?"

The older one, who had seen more than a hundred first-time fathers in her career, smiled sweetly and replied, "Just breathe, sir. Let's get these forms filled out, and I can show you where the waiting room is."

Manfred finished his cigarette and wandered back into the hospital, past the nurse's station, and down the hall to the waiting room. He had just seen Strauss about half an hour earlier, who told him everything and everyone was doing just fine.

Manfred's relief had been palpable. He knew the baby had not been due until around May first, but Dr. Strauss had assured him all was well.

"Don't forget, Mr. Amsel," the doctor had said, "due dates are not set in stone, merely educated guesses. Babies come when they are ready."

He'd only been back in the waiting room about two minutes when the nice nurse who had helped him with the paperwork appeared.

"Mr. Amsel," she called, smiling. "Let's go see your wife and son, shall we?"

It would be three days before Rose was released from the hospital. The labor had been hard on her slender frame, but she and the baby were both healthy. Manfred thought they made the most beautiful picture he'd ever seen, or ever would. He and Rose decided to name their precious gift Daniel.

***

Through the 1950's, Manfred Amsel had continued to gain respect from the students he taught at both Universities. While his curriculum at Humboldt was dictated not by the chancellors but by the Soviet-backed regime, he still managed to present the material in such a manner that kept the State happy but also expanded young minds to the idea that there was more than one way to view things. This was quite a balancing act, and he took pride in doing it well.

Only once had he let his personal passion answer for him.

One day in 1955, a young man in one of his discussion groups had become quite agitated and abruptly left the room. Manfred had encountered this young man several times during the semester and enjoyed the thoughtful and well-phrased contributions he made to various discussions. Manfred felt kindly toward him. The exchanges had always been pleasant, so the young man's reaction and sudden departure seemed completely out of character.

It was the day that another student had asked Manfred about his feelings on the Nazi party. Manfred, while taking care to phrase his response carefully, left little doubt for his listeners that he viewed the Nazi movement as a lethal cancer in the world that needed to be destroyed. The young man who suddenly bolted from the room was crimson with repressed rage, and Manfred never saw him at school again. His name was Adolf Werner.

Adolf Werner had been born in Berlin in 1934 to ardent Nazis. They lived comfortably as the third generation of Werners in the family home. His mother was a gifted seamstress who took great pride in making repairs and alterations to Nazi uniforms and insisted on naming her only child after the Fuhrer. Adolf's father was a lifelong friend and confidant of a ruthless man who would one day be prominent in the SS – Ernst Kaltenbrunner. Adolf simply called him Uncle Ernst.

The boy was preternaturally gifted with intelligence to the level of genius. In this vein, he and Manfred Amsel were not very far apart at all. But the similarity ended there. Manfred, along with his parents, loathed Hitler and his Nazis, whereas Adolf's parents signed him into the "Deutsches Jungvolk", the initial intake for German boys into the Nazi Party, as soon as he turned ten. Adolf was furious; he would rather have joined Hitler Youth straightaway to be closer to any real action, but one had to be at least fourteen for that group. He went above and beyond the required 'Nazified' educational curriculum and voraciously read anything and everything concerning the Nazi movement, taking especially to heart as gospel anything written or spoken by Hitler himself. This was encouraged by his parents, who saw in their son a great and dark possible successor to the Fuhrer. And when Adolf's father, on his less and less frequent trips home, would regale him with war stories, the boy was absolutely riveted.

Coupled with Adolf's gift of brilliance was an unfortunate tendency toward extreme sociopathic behavior. He could be as cruel and unfeeling as any hardened SS officer. At the tender age of six, he would befriend and then secretly inform on neighbors that he personally perceived to be unworthy or undesirable to the authorities, whether he had any proof against them or not. Then he would gleefully position himself to watch triumphantly as the families he was helping to destroy were rounded up and sent away, many to their deaths. The only thing keeping Adolf Warner from becoming another infamous Nazi monster was that he simply was not yet old enough to do widespread damage.

The fall of Hitler's regime in 1945 had not only felt like a personal loss to Adolf Werner, but like the snatching away of his birthright. He grieved for the Reich the way a normal eleven-year-old would grieve a close family member. His grief would turn to a dangerous, simmering anger lurking just below the surface of that blond hair, upturned pixie nose, and green eyes. The anger would harden into a profound rage when his father was hauled off by the Soviet invaders and eventually put to death for his role in the SS and for his refusal to renounce his political beliefs.

The Soviets simply did not think to look past the physical appearance, the outer shell of the SS officer's son; they only saw an eleven-year old, fair-haired boy. In their defense, on the surface the child's demeanor was average, like any other child caught in a post-war occupation. But this child's mask was superb, hiding a maniacally gifted mind, almost robotic lack of remorse or regret, and a twisted and bent soul well advanced beyond his body's eleven years. He would be satisfied with nothing less than the return of the Reich to its proper place. And so, Adolf hid himself in plain sight. He pretended to listen with rapt attention as the schooling he received from 1946 onward was increasingly overrun with Communist theory. He pretended to embrace the Soviet tormentors as saviors when all the while his psyche was berating them for the vermin he felt them to be.

Adolf started at Humboldt in 1954 and found the force-fed Communist doctrine was not as stifling in college as in primary school, but still definitely present. He continued his façade among other University students very successfully – at least until that day in 1955, when Manfred Amsel skewered his belief system through the heart, and Adolf's façade nearly cracked wide open. He strode quickly from the room, away from the blasphemer, trying to contain the erupting volcano in his head. Manfred Amsel had just unwittingly placed himself in Adolf's crosshairs for revenge. And, Adolf swore with a steely determination, it was not to be hastily enacted. No. The good professor would be brutally crucified when he least expected it.

***

Manfred, Rose, and Daniel came home from the hospital on the fifteenth of April, 1961. Always warm and inviting, the house that Manfred had spent many years in now seemed like a true home thanks to the presence of his wife's love and their little angel. He sensed his mother and father's presence, and his one regret in it all was that they did not live to see their grandson.

Manfred returned to teaching the following week, and although not as often as before, Rose would still accompany him to the American sector. Daniel's maternal grandparents enjoyed seeing Rose and the baby every chance they got. Through the summer, Rose occasionally spent the entire weekend with her family, while Manfred would travel back and forth as needed for classes. One such instance was the weekend of Friday August the eleventh. Manfred had planned on staying all weekend but had to return to the Soviet zone on Saturday for a conference at Humboldt University. Little Daniel was sick with colic, so Manfred hugged and kissed Rose gently, told her to stay and visit with her family, and to expect him back at her parents' house Sunday afternoon.

As usual, Manfred crossed back into East Berlin via public transport. He attended his conference on Saturday afternoon, which involved discussion on the upcoming fall curriculum and class schedules and ran late into the early evening. He made his way home, had a light, simple meal, did some reading in preparation for Monday's class over at Freie Universität in the American sector, and took two aspirin to ward off an approaching headache. He planned to sleep in a little, then rejoin his lovely bride and son at his in-law's house. As he drifted off to sleep, the world was as it had always been.

The same could not be said for when he awoke.

CHAPTER TWO

Manfred rose refreshed around ten a.m., with the aspirin taken the previous night having done a splendid job. He showered, shaved, and dressed, then quickly fixed himself a light brunch. Perhaps, he thought, little Daniel would be feeling better today, and they would be able to take a walk with the baby in the stroller later this evening when the temperature cooled a bit. Leaving the house around eleven, he decided the day was not unbearably warm, so he opted to walk rather than drive. Heading to the corner, he turned left onto Brunnenstrasse, and headed north toward Bernaur Strasse. Crossing Invalidenstrasse, he decided to stop and get a paper on his way to public transport, so he would have something to read that did not involve his career.

The paper was obviously Communistic in tone – the good folks running East Germany would have it no other way – but nonetheless, from time to time it contained articles meant to be taken seriously, that Manfred found amusing. He was making polite small talk with the elderly shopkeeper while he waited for his change. The old man asked him what he thought about the wire. Manfred had no clue what the man was talking about.

Alarm bells began to ring distantly in the back of his mind, but he dismissed them. *As loose as Russian soldiers' lips could be, he would surely have heard something...*

He said his goodbyes, and left, his step quickening all by itself.

As he continued to approach Bernaur Strasse and the Church of Reconciliation on his left, he was absolutely dumbfounded to see great, thick rolls of barbed wire running down the middle of the street, passing directly in front of the church. Armed guards stood every ten meters or so, watching construction workers drill holes in the cobbled street to add some sort of fortifying materials to the structure taking shape. Across this growing border was West Berlin, only one hundred yards away. It might as well as have been one mile.

Surely, Manfred thought, *this was some sort of ill-conceived joke. Who in their right mind would run barbed wire down a perfectly passable main thoroughfare?* But his heart told him this was no mere exercise. His stomach plunged to his feet as the implications of what he was seeing, but still could not believe, sank in.

He abruptly turned around, heading back toward his home. This time he turned right on Invalidenstrasse, crossed Chausseestrasse, and headed for the crossing into the Tiergarten district in the British zone. Upon reaching the border, he was crushed to see not only more wire, but more solid pieces already in place at this border intersection.

This border crossing was a large one for passing from East to West and, in this location, he saw crowds gathered on either side. The faces on the West side, painfully visible from his view, were contorted in anger and shouting insults eastward at the workers laying wire. The faces all around him on the East side were subdued, as much from the same shock he was feeling as the fact that armed men who looked as if they would enjoy firing their semi-automatic rifles were literally everywhere.

He and Klaus, his father-in-law, had had this discussion more than once. Klaus had previously wondered aloud exactly why the Soviet Zone in Berlin had not been cut off from the West along with the rest of its Zone in 1952. Manfred had personally believed that the Soviets would not be so audacious as to attempt to barricade more than ninety-six miles through the heart of the city itself.

As he was now learning with great personal distress, he had been wrong. His mind reeling, he slowly made his back way to his house. He sat numbly in the living room for a while before composing himself enough to turn on his Mambo portable radio. Although he could now not reach West Germany, West Germany could still reach him through the airwaves. He let the noise of 'Radio Free Berlin' pulse over him as he considered his next move.

In the American sector, Rose was absolutely frantic. A neighbor had been outside earlier that morning and came knocking on the door, babbling frantically about tanks. Klaus raced outside. Rose handed Daniel to her mother and followed her father out the door. They made their way toward Checkpoint Charlie – the crossing between the American and Soviet sectors of Berlin – and were completely amazed by what they saw. East German forces in Berlin had quite obviously been reinforced. Barbed wire was being placed along the East side border, along with menacing-looking men with huge weapons.

With tears in her eyes, Rose looked silently at her father, who took her hand, squeezed it tightly, and ever so slightly shook his head. Manfred would not be rejoining them, not today, possibly not ever again. The border closing that Klaus had wondered about for so long was now a reality.

***

The border closing had caught the average citizen in East Berlin and everyone in West Berlin completely by surprise, because at least this one time a secret plan by the Soviet-backed East German militia and leaders had been successfully kept a secret. Throughout that Sunday and Monday, West Germans who had been visiting in East Berlin over the weekend were allowed to return through specific checkpoints to the West, but not before their identity cards and any possessions they carried were scrutinized very carefully. Manfred began to hear reports that the rail lines and telephone lines – anything connecting East and West – had also been severed with the erection of the border.

He joined the throng on Monday and attempted to go through on foot into Tiergarten, in the British sector. He was told by the East German guards that his Freie Universität credentials had been suspended. He tried again to pass through Checkpoint Charlie into the American sector, and once again the East German guards turned him away. He appealed to the chancellors at Humboldt, to no avail. Manfred did not possess West German papers; his University credentials were his last best hope of making it through legally.

Finally, he decided this constituted enough of an emergency to get out the transmitter. He retrieved it from the false space he had added up in the loft, set it up, and sent a quickly worded and most definitely coded message to his old friend Max in the American sector. Manfred did not leave the transmitter on to receive one back; he did not expect to. His message had been for informational purposes only.

On Monday afternoon, Max Jones was summoned to the command post in the American sector.

"The Professor made contact, sir," the radio operator said. "It's coded, addressed to Jones, marked '*eyes only*'." The operator double-checked what he had written down to make sure he'd interpreted the signals correctly before handing the paper to Max.

Dismayed, Max looked down at the sheet. He and Manfred had spoken several times about what to do if an emergency arose. They had decided that Manfred would send a brief message. If he needed a response from the American sector, he would sign off with a particular set of symbols that indicated when he would be listening to receive a signal. If those symbols did not appear at the end of the message, it meant the signal was sent for information only and Manfred did not expect a reply.

This message contained no 'call me back' symbols, as Max and Manfred had jokingly called them. Max frowned. The sooner this could be decoded, the better. He needed to know what was happening, not just with a colleague, but with his friend. He took the message to a nearby desk and sat down with a clean notepad.

The cipher Manfred had been taught was a rotating one. In odd years, the beginning letter of the key to break the code corresponded with the fourth letter of the month the message was sent. In even years, it was the fifth letter. In the case of May, the default starting letter was 'Y', and in four-letter months, the letter moved to the first.

Setting his cipher key to 'U', the fourth letter in August in an odd year, Max transcribed the following: *"Garden fence /bad for gophers/ Kiss the flowers."* Manfred's message, in straightforward English, meant *"The border has been closed. I will go under it. Tell Rose for me."* Max strode from the room, the decoded message in his hand, to go tell Rose Amsel what was happening with her husband.

***

After the confrontation with Manfred Amsel on that cursed day in 1955, Adolf abandoned school entirely and focused on work and his hate. He spent the next six years existing as he had before college, on autopilot, moving through his day-to-day grind as a lowly janitor in one of the Socialist Unity Party's many buildings in East Berlin. He was invisible to and beneath those in power, so he easily gathered interesting bits of data from time to time.

He had known about the 1952 border closing around the entire Soviet sector of Germany before it happened. He'd also heard about what was going to happen in Berlin in August 1961, and frankly did not care much. He had already walled himself in. At this point he saw no reason why it should impact his plans and dreams. No one in the Party recognized his true nature, which was just as well.

Most nights Adolf spent pacing in his small and sparsely furnished apartment, ranting quietly to himself. When his mother became ill with cancer, he cared for her until her death in December 1961. Although the Soviet occupiers had nothing to do with his mother dying, he added his loss of her to their list of transgressions. Her death was the final blow that pushed him over the edge into carefully disguised insanity. The hate and frustration inside him grew daily, but to his great credit the surface remained, as ever, still and calm.

Adolf Werner was very much aware that nothing within the walls of academia or in his current life would help his beloved Reich return. All he needed, he thought desperately, was some sort of blueprint to follow, and he would have all the tools required to set the resurrection of the Nazi Party in motion. But in this new Communist state that would be next to impossible.

He had no one now to confide in. His mother was dead. He had long ago shut himself off from the very few friends he had made, fearing to trust anyone. He wished, yet again, that his father was still alive. Father would know what was to be done; he always had.

And then the thought, brilliant and warm and comforting, slipped into his head.

Had Mother not lovingly packed away Father's things? Had Mother not, with many tears, locked Father's trunk and asked Adolf to help her move it further back in the attic away from prying eyes? Adolf had only returned to live in his parents' home since his mother's death eight weeks before, and frankly had not thought about that great steamer trunk in years. Perhaps the answers he desperately needed could be found there.

He had nothing to lose by looking.

***

While Manfred had already decided the safest way across the Wall was underneath it, the group effort on the tunnel was pure luck. He had been walking past the Church on Bernaur one evening just after dusk on August twentieth when he happened to run into Wilhelm, one of his students. Wilhelm motioned Manfred to follow him.

Once they were both assured of not being seen or overheard, Wilhelm said quietly, "Hello, Professor. What brings you out this time of night?"

Manfred had been out scouting a logical location from which to begin digging the tunnel. But Manfred carefully replied, "Just taking a walk, I couldn't sleep."

Wilhelm leaned in a little closer and whispered, "Some of us are working together to find a way out to the West. We could use your help, Professor."

Manfred thought for a moment, then answered, "Let's meet on campus in my office; if anyone asks, we are forming a new discussion group. Tomorrow afternoon, say, around two?"

Wilhelm smiled, nodded, and faded into the night.

The following afternoon, the group met as planned. It consisted of Manfred and seven students, including Wilhelm and a very bright eighteen-year-old named Peter. They quietly discussed the border, how quickly it had gone up, and the possibility that it would continue to be fortified. This was extremely likely, given the fact that some East Germans had braved the wire already in broad daylight and in groups. The team needed to assume that more permanent structures would be put into place.

"Therefore, the easiest way to cross would not be through the gauntlet of walls and wires but passing underneath it. We need a tunnel, making sure we can camouflage the entrance extremely well," Manfred announced.

"What better place than a graveyard?" Wilhelm asked. "People venturing into the graveyard would not be unusual, visiting family plots and so on. Fresh earth or signs of digging will not be suspicious. As long as we're not all there together if we can help it, this might work."

Everyone agreed. After the initial dig, however, the hole would need to be camouflaged. The team all thought about this for a moment.

Peter smiled and said, "I've got it. How about a funeral arrangement, one of the really big ones? We don't have to buy one; maybe we can make something that looks like one, big enough to cover the hole. We wouldn't need to dig a grave-size hole. It could be smaller, right?"

Manfred smiled despite himself. Peter's enthusiasm was contagious.

"Brilliant idea, Peter. I think you just found a major piece of the puzzle for us," Manfred said.

Peter beamed.

"The two most important things," Manfred pointed out, "are that this tunnel will not happen overnight, and that it must be kept absolutely secret. Not even your family members must know about it until right before you use it to get out. If we're caught, we will be fortunate to only be jailed."

At this, all smiles faded. One look around the room at the seven young and somber faces told him they all understood and agreed. They worked out a rotating schedule, discussed a few more points, then closed the meeting, each heart now filled with hope and expectation of both hard work and a successful ending.

To make their efforts easier, and to enable more than one or two in the graveyard without arousing suspicion, Manfred went to the Church where he and Rose had been married and also had been attending services. He volunteered to maintain the graveyard and church grounds. He explained that he and some of his students wanted to help. The pastor was gracious and gladly accepted the offer – like many of the congregation, the groundskeepers had lived in the French district and could no longer reach the Church because of the Wall. The team could now travel to and from the Church grounds on a regular basis without raising too many questions.

The following week, work on the tunnel began. It was slow, but it had to be to keep from attracting attention. Team members would alternate working down in the tunnel to lengthen it and staying above ground to keep watch while mowing, raking, and weeding the graveyard. The team members were all extremely careful to be aware of their surroundings, not just at the tunnel site, but traveling to and from. These youngsters made Manfred's heart swell with pride. They somehow instinctively knew, without him having to say a word, to check behind them periodically for a tail as they traveled.

None of the team knew that Manfred was in fact an Allied spy in addition to being their professor, and they would never know. All the same, it pleased him to see how sharp and attentive they were to details that could save their lives.

Bit by bit, the tunnel grew. Thanks to growing up with a mathematical wizard for a father, Manfred had been able to calculate the dimensions necessary to complete the task. The surface hole was around three feet in diameter and was camouflaged brilliantly by the funeral arrangement Peter had suggested. The tunnel was approximately five feet down, and gradually widened to five feet at the base of the entrance hole to provide some sort of ability to maneuver. This was mainly for the Professor's benefit as he was the only one over five feet seven inches tall.

The tunnel could not just travel the three-hundred feet or so to the other side of the Wall by the Church, then just pop up. One, there was no cover on the West side right across from the church, only open street and sidewalk. The East Germans couldn't be counted on not to fire into West Berlin if they saw someone magically rise from beneath the street. Two, digging upward by hand through cement or cobblestones would be extremely difficult. No, the tunnel had to run approximately one-third of a mile, coming up into a little park area in the Hiedestrasse area in the Tiergarten district. The trees there would provide better cover.

Regular checks using a compass were made, both above ground and in the tunnel, to ensure that the tunnel was proceeding in the right direction. Progress was coming along nicely, given the fact that all they had to dig with were ordinary gardening tools. At the rate they were working, Manfred estimated the tunnel would be complete sometime in August 1962, provided there were no complications.

The diameter of the tunnel itself grew to roughly four feet tall and wide, big enough to travel through on hands and knees. It was being reinforced along the sides every two or three feet with wood or bricks or whatever the team could find. Figuring out new and subtle ways to disperse all the earth being moved was becoming more difficult as well. This dilemma and the lack of adequate shoring materials were both solved one afternoon when Manfred suggested to the pastor that planting flowerbeds along the entire front, sides, and walkways of the church grounds would add a nice touch.

The pastor smiled, leaned in, and whispered conspiratorially, "Manfred, you're a good man. I've known for some time what you and your young people are up to in the graveyard. I have been meaning to suggest you add more landscaping efforts to strengthen your cover story. Now, child, you must be getting low on shoring materials. You'll find several items in the basement that I believe will be useful, extra building materials from the church repairs in 1948. Take anything you need."

Manfred was temporarily stunned. "Thank you, Father," he said, slightly flushed. "I didn't want to involve you directly in case we were found out; I wanted to protect you."

To which the elderly pastor replied solemnly, "My soul will go to God when I die, regardless of how I die; in that I am both protected and comforted. Let me know, Manfred, if I can help in any other way."

Toward the end of the tunnel's creation, in mid-1962, a second Wall began to be added to the border, as Manfred and his team had forecasted. This one was comprised of concrete blocks but was being put up slower than the first barrier had been. The team knew that as the workers building this second Wall moved closer to Bernaur Strasse and the Church, more discretion would be vital to keep from being caught so close to success.

***

Adolf leaned back, sweaty and muscles aching with effort, to take a little break. It was hot and stuffy up here, but worth it. Fortunately, he was almost done and would not have to brave this attic in the roiling heat of the impending summer – it was bad enough in May. His hunch to check his father's old things had finally paid off. Three generations' worth of items in the attic seemed to have multiplied on their own at least twice since his last visit up those creaky old stairs in 1947. Mother had managed to accumulate quite a bit more in the last fifteen years. It had taken him almost a month to carefully clear a path to the old trunk put away so many years ago. Along the way he had found a treasure trove of strange and wonderful things, including some hideous baby clothes of his. God only knew what Mother had been thinking, keeping some of it.

At long last he had spied his quarry in the back corner, protected by a very thick layer of dust and cobwebs. Breaching its outer defenses, he cursed when he realized the key was nowhere to be found. The lock was old but sturdy, and thwarted various attempts to open it. Finally, he heaved and grunted and maneuvered the big trunk around where he could access the hinges on the back. These proved to be more vulnerable and yielded to persistence with a chisel and hammer.

His breath had caught as the faint odor of his father's aftershave wafted up from the old greatcoat. Memories flooded like a monsoon. Overcome for a moment, he had to pause to let the storm pass. Recollections of sitting with his parents by the fire, entranced by his father's adventures on behalf of the Reich, seemed like they happened only yesterday. He traced his fingers over the collar of his father's greatcoat, where his mother had proudly attached the swastikas. Removing each item from its resting place lovingly, carefully, Adolf began to work his way through the trunk's contents.

Toward the bottom, he spied what looked like a sheaf of papers bound with twine. His pulse quickened as he reached forward to take his future out of hiding. A quick glance confirmed the documents were in his father's handwriting. The first page was addressed to Adolf himself and was dated May nineteenth, 1945. But the rest of the writing was gibberish, groups of numbers and slash marks – a three-digit number, then a slash, then another three-digit number; he estimated there to be around a hundred such pages, written on both sides. Adolf remembered his father's demeanor well enough to know this was not accidental. It had to mean something, something extremely important, or Father would not have bothered to encode it. If he could just figure out how to break the code, he would have all the answers he needed.

Reluctantly, he set his newfound treasure to one side and carefully continued looking through his father's things, including the Luger Uncle Ernst had given Father as a gift. And finally, reaching the bottom of the trunk, he saw it, etched into the wood. A father-to-son family joke of sorts in the past, now a beacon, lighting the way to his dreams. Two simple yet powerful words left by his father, the meaning of which was crystal clear to him.

Family Bible.

Adolf brushed sweat and cobwebs from his face and laughed, quite possibly his first genuine laugh since he was eleven, before his world had shattered. He knew how to break the code. Turning to his left, he searched back through the pile of things he'd set to the side and pulled it triumphantly from the stack – the autographed copy of *Mein Kampf*, his father's most treasured possession. He replaced everything in the trunk except the papers and the book, saving the gun until last for easier access.

Smiling and whistling softly to himself, he headed downstairs to recharge with a shower, food, and a drink. He had work to do.

CHAPTER THREE

On the evening of August twelfth, 1962, Adolf and Manfred were both jubilant, but for very different reasons.

Manfred crawled back toward the tunnel entrance in the graveyard, pleased with himself and with his students. They were finished. It had taken the group just shy of a year, but finally the door was open that led to freedom if their luck continued to hold. He silently thanked the weather in advance for its cooperation – the evenings were projected to be overcast all week, which would decrease the chances of being silhouetted by moonlight.

Part of him wanted to just go ahead and make the crossing and never look back, taking all his students at the same time. But six people traveling as a group after dark would draw unnecessary attention and was too big a risk. His concern for his students and his certainty that their exits needed to be well planned overrode his desire to kiss his wife and hold his child. A few days more, he told himself. He needed to take certain things with him, and he needed to let Max know he was coming. Two students had used the tunnel successfully tonight. The others would attempt it in pairs over the next three nights. He and Peter would try to cross on Thursday, provided everything went as planned.

***

Adolf lowered his pen, picked up his glass, toasted his surroundings, and exhaled in triumph. Ten weeks of long nights had paid off. The translation was finished. In his hands he held a complete manifesto for the resurrection of the Nazi party – a plan that could be enacted anywhere provided conditions were right – and instructions for something called 'schweres Wasser' – heavy water. Adolf had no idea what that meant, but it must be important to be included in these documents. The papers his father had left for him were priceless. Once the deciphering was done, Adolf was able to read the documents in their entirety. The first page, the one that had addressed him directly, turned out to be in part a letter from his father explaining the history of how the documents came to be.

His father had been a close friend of Ernst Kaltenbrunner, who was not only very highly placed in the SS, but also a favorite of Hitler himself. As a result, Ernst was entrusted with several sensitive manuscripts just after Allied forces entered Germany. When Berlin fell to the Soviets on the eighth of May, 1945, Kaltenbrunner found himself on the run, heading south to avoid capture. He in turn gave the documents to Adolf's father, who immediately transcribed a coded version and then destroyed the originals. His father wrote that it grieved him to burn such visionary texts written by the Fuhrer himself, but it was necessary.

Transferring the documents was fortuitous – Kaltenbrunner was captured by Allied forces on May the fifteenth and was tried and executed at Nuremberg in October, 1946. And although Adolf's father had no way of knowing at the time, the destruction of the originals was also fortuitous, as he would be hauled away and executed by Soviet forces before summer's end.

But there was more. The letter revealed his father's intention to travel with Uncle Ernst via a pre-arranged transport to South America; they were to meet other Nazi leaders there. "*Adolf,*" his father wrote, "*with any luck you are reading this and will join me there.*" It went on to mention a code phrase, contact names, and rendezvous points, both at the German border and at his destination, and that further instructions would be waiting for him once he arrived.

Adolf cursed, throwing his glass in frustration. Obviously the 'further instructions' his father mentioned never happened, and the border contact here in Germany his father had written about was no good either – it was a location in Communist-held territory. Even if he could find the individual, getting out of East Germany would be almost impossible. But maybe, just maybe, he could follow the old thread enough to find a new way to his brethren.

Adolf studied the translated papers exhaustively over the next three days, committing them to memory as much as possible. Then he followed in his father's footsteps and placed the translated pages and the personal letter from his father into the fire, one by one. But he knew that with police patrols becoming more aggressive in the Mitte District, he would not be able to keep the coded documents in his possession for long either. Being caught with items so obviously encrypted would spell huge trouble with the authorities. But where to hide them? He needed anonymity just as much as security.

Walking home from work on Thursday afternoon, he found the solution to his problem. As he passed the Church of Reconciliation, he heard a great deal of commotion. It was workmen putting pieces of the new Wall into place. Traveling around to the southwest side of the church, he carefully peeked around the corner. As he suspected, the new Wall was being erected to run along the southernmost edge of the graveyard.

He observed the work for a few moments while a plan was forming in his mind. Unlike the first barrier of wooden posts and wire, this new structure was being installed to be more permanent – poured concrete as a base, then concrete bricks set into it and atop one another. And, he noted, the workers left their mixer and wheelbarrow sitting there as they left the site for the day.

If he absolutely had to, he could hide the coded papers within the Wall itself! No one would find them, and even if someone did, they would not be able to trace the papers back to him or be able to break the code.

***

In the American sector, Max Jones was summoned to the radio room at five-thirty p.m. on an otherwise quiet Thursday. The night operator verified she had written down the symbols correctly, then passed him the paper.

"From the Professor, sir. It's his call sign," she remarked. "Three groupings of letters, two sets of three, then a set of seven."

Max sat down, turned his cipher key to the correct letter, and transcribed the message that resulted in a huge smile spreading across his face: "*see you tonight.*"

***

Manfred switched off his radio and put it back in its hiding place for what he hoped would be the last time. He walked down the stairs, and for a moment he stood in silence in the living room, recognizing the irony of the situation. Manfred now knew exactly what his mother had felt the day they left for London so many years ago. He sighed and continued toward his bedroom to gather only what he absolutely had to take with him. That took all of ten minutes.

He went to the kitchen, made a sandwich, and poured himself a drink. Taking a seat on his sofa, he picked up a magazine. He glanced at the clock and sighed again. Two minutes past six. Now that he was so close to seeing Rose again, time seemed to have stopped altogether. He wasn't supposed to meet Peter at the Church until eight.

It would be a long two-hour wait.

***

Adolf placed his precious documents into two successively bigger envelopes, then wrapped it all in waxed paper as best he could, taking care to ensure all the ends were well sealed. It might be a long time before he would see them again, and they would serve him no purpose if they were damaged.

"I hope those lazy dolts left the wheelbarrow," he said aloud to no one. It would make the task of stashing his valuables a little simpler. He retrieved his jacket from the front hall, tucked his package carefully inside his waistband at the small of his back so it would not be visible, zipped up his jacket, locked his front door, and stepped out into a moonless night.

***

By seven forty-five p.m., Manfred could wait no longer. He gathered his satchel, jacket, and hat, and cast one last look around his family home. It was time. He could feel his pulse quicken as he locked the front door for the final time and walked down the sidewalk. The Church was five blocks away. He would spend a few minutes with the pastor and wait for Peter there.

***

Drawing his breath in sharply, Adolf shrank back into the shadows. A figure was walking down the other side of the street, coming closer and closer. Was it the police? Adolf's heart felt like it would explode, and his mind raced to come up with a logical reason why he would be out walking at this time of night. Then his brain processed the information his eyes were seeing – it was another civilian. The man was carrying some sort of briefcase. When he passed under one of the streetlamps in front of the old church the man happened to glance upward, as if he felt raindrops.

Adolf saw his face and smiled an evil smile. It was that damn know-it-all professor who'd dared to speak harshly of the Reich. That man's name and face had been etched by hatred into his memory. With a rage pounding in his head that suffocated any sense of self-awareness, Adolf began to cross the street.

***

Manfred paused outside the church to put on his jacket. He was beginning to feel a mist falling. Suddenly, the hair stood on the back of his neck – he was being watched. Following his instincts, he turned sharply to his left, gazing across the street. Raising his hand to shield his eyes from the streetlight, he could just make out a silhouette coming toward him. Sensing the figure approaching was not a friendly one, Manfred walked briskly up the steps of the church and opened the door. From the doorway he risked a look back. The mysterious figure was nowhere to be seen.

***

Adolf had to sit on the curb for a moment to let the fire in his temples subside. As he slowly reined in his temper, his mind cleared. He had a job to do, first and foremost. Payback could come after – immediately after, as far as he was concerned. *Why not tonight?* He decided to place his treasure as planned in the Wall, then position himself to wait for Manfred to come out of his sanctuary. *Yes, that would do nicely.*

He stood up, looked around to make sure he was not being watched himself, and surreptitiously made his way into the graveyard with a small flashlight. He found that, once again, the men building the Wall had neglected to clean the site at the end of the workday. Not only was the wheelbarrow and hand mixer left behind, but he was also rewarded with half a bag of concrete powder and a small bucket. Now all he needed was water. He had noticed that afternoon that just next to the back door of the church was a little spigot. Casting his flashlight around, he retrieved the bucket and started toward the church door.

***

Inside the pastor's office, Manfred was standing at the window overlooking the graveyard, only half-listening to the Father's conversation attempts. The pastor assumed it was due to nerves about making the crossing. But the scene that had unfolded outside was what had the professor distracted. Pushing the incident out of his mind, Manfred turned to give his full attention to the pastor, who was saying, "Everyone has made it through to the other side safely as far as I know. I believe it is just you that remains."

"No," Manfred replied, gazing out the window. "I have one more student over here. He will be traveling with me tonight."

The church bell rang. He startled and went on.

"Curious that he is not here. We were supposed to meet an hour ago, and that young man is usually quite punctual. I fear something has happened to him, Father," Manfred said with concern. Turning to face the pastor, Manfred missed seeing Adolf's flashlight beam by the narrowest of margins.

***

The water spigot happened to be located under the very window that Manfred was in front of. Adolf froze, taking care to turn off his flashlight, and waited until the figure in the window retreated from view. It seemed an eternity. Adolf needed to move quickly. He turned on the water as quietly as possible and positioned the bucket so the water would cascade down the side to minimize the splashing and the noise. This accomplished, he turned off the water, turned his flashlight back on, and carried the bucket back toward the far end of the graveyard.

He set the bucket down, dumped the concrete powder into the hand mixer, added some of the water, and began to turn the crank, immediately wincing at the noise. He realized it would be less efficient but safer to mix the concrete by hand; as quiet as the night was, he just couldn't risk the sound of the mixer. He looked around and found a mason's trowel. That would have to do. Adolf stirred the mixture until it was just about the right consistency. He slid the documents out from his waistband and set them and the flashlight on the ground, directing the beam at the Wall so he could see.

***

Manfred had turned back to the window and was startled to see what looked like a light shining from somewhere within the graveyard, very close to the tunnel entrance. He retrieved the Walther from his satchel, loaded it, and put in his jacket pocket. Then he motioned to the pastor to join him at the window and pointed to what had caught his attention.

"I think we ought to go out the front and walk around the side of the building, Father," said Manfred.

"Hopefully it's Peter out there, but if it's not him, then it would probably be to our advantage to not be seen at first. It could be a police patrol."

The pastor was concerned but in agreement.

***

Pushing the mixer over to the base of the Wall, Adolf poured a little of the concrete into the raw section of base trench the Wall builders had dug out in preparation for the next day's work. Completely absorbed in his work, he was oblivious to Manfred and the pastor quietly approaching. Adolf placed his package on the wet concrete, taking care to center it, then began to add more concrete very carefully until his treasure was buried about four inches deep. He used the remainder of the concrete he'd mixed to fill in the rest of the space, then smoothed the surface with the trowel. When he was finished, the little section he had poured came level to the existing Wall base – absolutely perfect.

Satisfied at last that the papers were safely tucked away, he took a switchblade from his pocket and etched two slightly curved grooves into both the hardening concrete and the lowest block next to it in the existing Wall. This would serve as a marker, the best one he could come up with that would not be obvious to anyone else. He checked his watch – nine thirty-one.

Almost done here, Adolf thought with a grim smile, *and then I can visit with the Professor.* He picked up his flashlight, stood up, and brushed himself off. Turning around, he nearly jumped out of his skin. He was face to face with Manfred and an elderly man he assumed to be the pastor of the church.

Manfred was shocked to see his old student standing before him with clenched fists and a look on his face that would have frightened the Devil himself. Their eyes met for a long moment.

"Adolf, isn't it? Adolf Werner?" Manfred asked softly.

Adolf glowered silently at them and said nothing. But his grip tightened on the knife still in his hand, and his mind went into overload trying to ascertain how he could gain an advantage. The raw seething rage that threatened to consume him made it difficult to maintain his mask of normalcy.

Then the pastor stepped forward and asked, "What in the world were you burying, my son?"

In that instant, Adolf reacted. The simple question asked made it clear that he'd been seen, been caught. He could leave no witnesses, especially since they knew his name. He quickly stepped forward toward Manfred, the arm holding the knife extended in front of him, intending to ram it through the blasphemer's heart. Manfred's hand went toward his pocket to withdraw his gun.

But the pastor instinctively stepped in front of Manfred to protect him. His frail body absorbed the full force of steel tearing into flesh and muscle. With a piercing scream, the pastor slumped downward, convulsed twice, and was still. Adolf stepped back, momentarily stunned. Without taking his eyes off Adolf, Manfred bent down to check the old man for a pulse and found none – the knife had destroyed the aorta.

The pastor's cry had carried on the still night air and caught the attention of a rookie policeman passing in front of the church on his very first solo patrol. Nervously, he drew his weapon, turned on his flashlight, and began to come around the side of the church to investigate.

Manfred and Adolf both saw the flicker of a light approaching. Adolf pocketed his knife as quickly as he could and slipped around the corner of the unfinished Wall. Manfred spun on his heel and headed straight for the tunnel ten feet away. Lifting the wreath, he wriggled under it and scrambled to replace it to properly cover the entrance. He settled it back into place just in time. He could hear slow, methodical footsteps close by. Then they stopped for a moment and were replaced with retching sounds. The policeman had obviously found the body. The footsteps started again, retreating very quickly.

Manfred realized the officer was returning to a callbox to inform dispatch about what he had found. Praying that his friend would rest in peace, Manfred turned on his flashlight and began the crawl to freedom with a heavy heart. He was also still extremely concerned about Peter. Hopefully the tunnel would remain undiscovered and Peter would still be able to use it.

Adolf had full view of both the policeman's movements and Manfred disappearing into the ground. When the cop went off to call in about the body, Adolf reappeared and stood over the pastor, feeling strangely satisfied. It was the first time he had killed, and he liked the intense sensations that came with it.

The shaky, bouncing light coming back toward him tempered his adrenalin rush. He once again slipped around the Wall and into the shadows as the body was examined, photographed, and removed from the scene by the mortuary crew. A perfunctory search of the area was made by the inexperienced officer and consisted mainly of wandering among the headstones for about five minutes before leaving.

Finally, Adolf had the graveyard to himself again. He knew exactly where he wanted to go, but he needed to make a quick detour first. Carefully, stealthily, he made his way back to his house. He went to the steamer trunk to retrieve and load the Luger. He picked up the gun and was stopped in his tracks by what was underneath it. The swastikas on his father's greatcoat seemed to stand out, call to him, even more than the day he first went through the trunk.

It hit him then – following the professor, going into West Berlin, would make it even more difficult to resurrect the Reich; that half of the city was surrounded with walls, guards, and Soviet territory. From East Berlin he could more easily reach the coast. He closed his eyes as his head and heart waged a mighty war within him. He wanted to feel the professor's blood on his hands, see with his own eyes the man's torment and death. Equally strong was the passion and desire to restore Hitler's legacy to its proper place.

Adolf went back downstairs to his room and grabbed his hiking pack. He placed his father's book in the bottom, then layered a few articles of clothing and toiletries to conceal it. A small loaf of bread, a sausage, a small wheel of cheese, and a canteen of water were added from the kitchen. Lastly, he opened his sideboard cupboard, brought out three old jars, and emptied them of their contents – roughly a year's salary that he'd saved up over time. He put as much as he could into his jeans pockets and the rest went into his backpack.

Placing the gun under his jacket and the hiking pack on his shoulders, he left his home without locking the door and returned to the graveyard. He crept over to the area where he had seen Manfred disappear, found the tunnel entrance, and removed the wreath. He stood as if at a crossroads, staring grimly into the hole, head and heart still at war...

***

By his estimation, Manfred had entered the tunnel sometime around nine forty-five; he had no idea what time it was now. As he crawled, his mind wandered. He didn't understand why Peter had not shown up. He also didn't understand the level of venom that Adolf had stared at him with. He remembered the day that Adolf had abruptly left class, but that was five or six years ago at least. Surely the young man was not still that upset over a simple group discussion.

More importantly, what the hell had Adolf been burying in the graveyard? Whatever it was, he'd been more than willing to kill for it...

***

As the church bell marked midnight, Adolf descended into the tunnel with a wolfish smile. He had made his choice. The hunt was on.

***

Manfred took his first steps onto West Berlin soil in over a year just after twelve-thirty a.m. on August the sixteenth. He had made it to the British sector. As he looked eastward, he hoped and prayed for Peter's safety and success. Then, getting his bearings, he set out for the American zone and Rose and Daniel.

*****

Fifty yards in, Adolf knew he'd made a huge error. A panic had started to set in that was making it extremely difficult to breathe. This was his first encounter with a dark, enclosed space, and he was surprised to find that it absolutely terrified him. He wanted to continue, to find the Professor and kill him, but his mind and body simply refused to cooperate. He finally managed to turn himself around in the small passageway and began crawling as fast as he could back toward open sky.

After what seemed like an eternity, he reached the gaping mouth of the tunnel and launched himself upward with a mighty effort. Freeing himself at last from his living grave, he lay on his back beside the cavern that had almost swallowed him, drawing in great gulps of night air. Gradually, the smothering panic subsided, and he regained his wits. He was able to stand up, discovering that although his legs were still shaking, they would indeed hold his weight. Moving on autopilot, he headed for home. The professor would have to wait until Adolf could find another way past the Wall.

*****

Back in the church graveyard at first light, a chastened rookie officer and the superintendent of the watch had returned to the scene with more men and lights to conduct a decent search. The tunnel entrance was now plainly visible and was discovered in short order. A guard was posted, and by seven a.m. the Wall builders had a new assignment – sealing the tunnel opening with concrete.

*****

The next morning, August seventeenth, Rose and Manfred were sitting side by side and hand in hand in her parents' living room as Daniel played with blocks in the floor. Klaus came in and in a solemn tone said, "Manfred, there's something you need to see."

Leaving their son with Emilie, they followed him outside and down the street toward Checkpoint Charlie, where a large crowd was gathering. Manfred wept as he recognized his student, Peter, pleading for help and bleeding to death from gunshot wounds in 'no-man's land', mere yards from the freedom of West Berlin.

SECTION TWO: A NEW START –

1962- 1997

CHAPTER FOUR

That evening, Manfred sat in the Meyer's living room with sixteen-month-old Daniel sleeping soundly in his arms. Watching his son dream, he marveled again at how much the child had grown in the time they had been apart.
"Never again," he whispered as he lowered his head to lightly kiss the baby's forehead. "Never again will I miss your birthday."
Daniel sighed in his sleep and snuggled closer in response.

Manfred was unaware that Rose had been standing in the doorway, watching the scene with misty eyes. "You won't have to, my love," she said, her voice thick with emotion. She crossed the room to sit beside her husband.

"Rose, we need to talk about something," Manfred said softly, so as to not wake the baby. "Max will be returning to America tomorrow. He's retiring from the Army and transferring into a government agency, and he's asked me to come and work for him. I told him you and I would have to discuss it. I know how close you are to your parents; you know I love them like my own. There's room for them to come with us if they wish. And my first priority is to make you happy. I know Germany is our home, Rose. But I honestly don't know if I can handle..." He trailed off as his eyes teared up and his voice broke. He took a deep breath, then continued. "I don't want to have to watch another person die senselessly, like Peter did today," he finished, his eyes dark with sorrow.

It broke her heart to see such grief on her husband's face. Rose placed her hand gently on Manfred's cheek and replied, "And you do make me happy. Manfred, my home is wherever you and Daniel are. We shall ask Mother and

Father if they want to come, of course. But I will go with you to America regardless of what they decide."

At dinner, Manfred and Rose talked with Klaus and Emilie about making the trip to America. Klaus leaned back slightly in his chair, furrowed his brow, then turned to his wife and asked, "What do you think?"

Emilie paused, glanced lovingly at her grandchild for a moment, and said, "It is an easy choice. We are a family. Families love and support one another. We have all been through so much here. Perhaps America is a good place for a new start – for all of us."

Klaus reached for her hand and kissed it.

The following afternoon, Max Jones, the Meyers, and the Amsels were in Tempelhof district, strapping themselves into their seats on a United States Air Force C-130. It was safer than attempting a commercial carrier. Soviet fighters had been menacing civilian aircraft flying in and out of West Berlin for years. Only Max had flown before and knew what to expect. The others were making their maiden voyage through the air and were extremely nervous. Over the whine of the engines, Max tried his best to reassure the group that everything would be fine.

Clasping hands tightly, each family member closed their eyes and prayed as the plane shuddered and shimmied and then took to the skies.

Putting West Berlin behind them, they leveled off and traveled roughly ninety minutes southwest toward Frankfurt in the American zone of Germany before turning slightly to the west. The journey continued for another seventy minutes before the plane began to approach Heathrow airport. Emilie yelped and clutched her husband's arm as the plane descended, and although Klaus was trying to keep his composure, he was turning an interesting shade of green. Manfred and Rose each snuggled closer to Daniel, who was sandwiched between them, and who was handling this new experience better than any of the grownups – he was sound asleep.

The passengers' relief was palpable when the aircraft touched ground lightly and came to a smooth stop. Max was unable to stop himself as his ragged group shrugged out of their seat belts. "Wasn't that delightful?" he queried, with a mischievous gleam in his eye.

Emilie turned to him and with a very small voice and a wan smile replied, "It was lovely, thank you, and I hope to never, ever do it again."

Max chuckled, and said with heartfelt sincerity, "Ma'am, welcome to London."

***

While Manfred and his family were surviving their first plane ride, Adolf was walking through the woods about seventy-seven miles south of Wittenberge.

After the attempt at the tunnel went horribly wrong, he had made his way home, frustrated with and ashamed of himself. He fell, fully clothed and emotionally raw, into his bed and slept a full sixteen hours. When he woke, he was his old self again, and was determined to take some sort of lesson from what had transpired. He was also ravenously hungry. As he made his way to the kitchen, he replayed the confrontation in the graveyard over and over in his mind, this time removing emotion from the equation and viewing it purely as a strategic analysis.

Of course, it went wrong, he thought as his hands busied themselves making a sandwich. *It was going to. I didn't hear them approach.* Lesson One: Be aware of your surroundings. *I telegraphed my intentions with the knife.* Lesson Two: If at all possible, catch your prey unaware.

Next, he took a hard look at what had happened to him in the tunnel. It was the one time he had felt complete and utter terror. He never wanted to feel it again. But it taught him Lesson Three: Expect the unexpected.

Lastly, the whole experience had taught him Lesson Four: The value of patience, logic, and staying the course.

He had let emotion overrule the intellect and common sense that needed to prevail to pull off reviving the Reich. Adolf realized his main objective needed to be, first and foremost, rebuilding the glory of the old ways. And that meant personal agendas such as dealing with the Professor would be random moments of opportunity, an added bonus, not a priority.

He ate, showered, shaved, and changed into comfortable walking gear for August – jeans, a t-shirt layered under a lightweight long-sleeve shirt, a light jacket, and his hiking boots. He checked the supplies again in his knapsack, adding his flashlight and extra batteries, a compass, a lighter, and some raisins. Then he sat down to pass the time until darkness fell by cleaning the Luger. That accomplished, he set the gun on the table and moved over to the couch, turning on the radio.

At some point, Adolf dozed and dreamed. He saw a structure rising magnificently from a barren wasteland. He saw himself standing at its entrance, dressed in full Kreigsmarine uniform, addressing a crowd that stood transfixed by his every word. And he saw a child, with hair so blond it looked white and unreadable eyes of slate gray. In his dream he reached and took the child's hand, and they turned and walked together into the massive building.

He awoke, snapping back to consciousness, every detail of the dream so vividly burned into his memory that he looked down at his hand, expecting to see it clasped around a very small one. It was an omen, a good one, he felt sure of it. Slowly, he arose and stretched, looking at the clock on the mantle. Eleven twenty-seven p.m. Time to go. He secured the pistol at the small of his back, gathered up his knapsack and looked around at his childhood home. He felt no sorrow in leaving. The future was not here.

Closing his front door softly, Adolf turned and began the long and lonely walk toward Wittenberge, one-hundred and nine miles to the northwest.

***

The Meyers and the Amsels stayed in London overnight, then boarded the first of a two-plane, two-day journey to the United States. Emilie was at first unwilling to even consider flying ever again. But Max reassured her that commercial aircrafts were much more comfortable for passengers than were military transports.

"You've been through the worst of it, my dear," he said, patting Emilie's hand. "The rest of your journey will resemble traveling by train."

Luckily for Max, he proved to be right. The flights from London to Glasgow to Dulles International Airport were each as smooth as could be, for which they were all profoundly grateful. Two Agency cars and drivers met them at the airport and drove them the eighteen miles to Manassas, Virginia, where their new lives awaited.

As the car turned into an older and very beautiful neighborhood, Max said, "We've arranged housing for you to help you get settled. I took the liberty of having the place furnished. Of course, you can stay as long as you like; if you decide to move to another place, that's fine too, Manfred. Whatever we can do to help."

Just then, the car slowed and made a left turn onto Battle Street, pulling into a long driveway. The old-fashioned colonial beckoned to them, welcoming them.

Rose's smile was instant and brilliant. "Oh, it's lovely," she exclaimed. Talking excitedly, Rose and her mother went from room to room in the three-story home. Klaus and Manfred were particularly taken with the finished basement. And the house seemed custom made for them — a spacious and airy kitchen, ample space to gather as a family, and three bedrooms, each with its own bath. Traveling through the back door revealed a huge, lush lawn with trees and neatly tended flowerbeds, and a porch that ran the entire length of the house.

Max leaned against the wall by the front door, smiling and waiting patiently. Once everyone was gathered in the front hall again, he said, "Will it do?"

Manfred walked over, shook his hand and said, "Absolutely."

"Very well, then." Max handed Manfred the keys to the house. "Take the next two days to relax and just enjoy your family. The rest of your things are in transit and should be here sometime tomorrow. I'm sure Rose and Emilie will want to set their new home in order." The ladies beamed.

Max continued. "Manassas is a lovely town with friendly people. Ben, one of the drivers outside, was born and raised here; he will be available to you until we can line up a Company car for you. He can show you around town and will take you wherever you want to go."

And to Manfred directly, he said, "I'll be by to pick you up bright and early Thursday morning for work."

***

Adolf had been walking for four days and guessed that within another day's time he would be in Wittenberge. He had been pacing himself – a comfortable strolling gait for about ten hours a day. So far, he had been very lucky. Once he'd gotten out of Berlin, he had been able to stay on or close to the road; there were very few people out here. Evidently, any Soviet troops or police authorities in the area had more important things to tend to besides manning a desolate stretch of farming road. But he still kept his awareness sharp as he walked, prepared to hide in the trees at a moment's notice.

The weather had been cooperating nicely; not nearly as hot as he anticipated it would be during the day, and comfortably cool at night. And sleeping under the stars was strangely calming. He had lain on his back and counted them last night until he drifted off. When he woke at first light, he felt more rested than he had in years.

As he walked along, he began to hear sounds of people nearby. Rounding the bend, he spied a pond just off to the left and heard the delighted squeals and laughter of children. The four of them saw him and waved. He slowed his pace and waved back but did not stop.

Around another bend was a crossroad angling off sharply to the right. He stopped, set down his pack, retrieved his compass, and studied it. Nodding in satisfaction, he put the compass in his pocket, took a quick drink from his canteen, picked up his pack, and headed up the path veering right. Twenty minutes later, a farmer with a wagon full of produce asked he could use a lift. They arrived in Wittenberge just after five p.m. Adolf thanked the man, descended from the cart, and set off in search of a meal and a bed. He found both in a small boarding house and settled in for the night.

In the morning, he asked the widow running the boarding house if there were any vehicles for rent in the small town. After receiving an amused look, he was directed down the street to an old bicycle shop. *Better this than walking another eighty miles*, he thought. He picked the least worn-out of the lot and bought it outright. It had a small basket attached directly behind the seat that held his hiking pack perfectly. Right next to the bicycle shop was a little general store. He went in and bought more sausages, cheese, and raisins to replenish his supplies. Storing them in his pack, Adolf climbed aboard to continue his journey toward Wismar and, hopefully, his contact.

Even with the bike, it was another two days before he reached his destination. His backside hurt from not having ridden so much since he was a child. He was tired, dirty, and hungry. His leg muscles screamed as he made his way up a steep hill. Reaching the top, he stopped and blinked twice as if he'd seen a mirage.

He had made it. The road sloped downward leading into the town; from his vantage point he could smell the salt of the ocean, perhaps five or six miles past Wismar. *Time to pull the old thread and see where it leads*, he thought. He leaned forward slightly and let gravity pull him, coasting down the hill. It was August the twenty-

third, a full week since he'd left his house in the Mitte
district of East Berlin.

***

Half a world away, Manfred was sitting in the guest chair
across from Max's desk in CIA headquarters in Langley,
Virginia. They'd not yet had a full debriefing regarding
the night of Manfred's escape into the West.

"Well, Max, where we do start?" Manfred asked.

"Tell me again about the young man in the graveyard.
You said his name was.... Adolf, correct?" Max asked,
searching his memory.

"That's correct. Adolf Werner," Manfred replied, and
relayed everything he knew or could remember about the
young man, from the time Adolf attended his classes until
the night in the graveyard.

Max stood and began to walk around the room,
talking as he went. "You said he got angry with you that
day in class. What specifically was the topic of the group
discussion that day?"

Manfred responded, "If I recall correctly, we were
talking about literature from different cultures. Somehow
the conversation worked around to political parties and
how their viability is directly impacted by their leaders. I
remember saying something along the lines of some of
them being doomed experiments, destined to fail.
Another of my students asked for an example, and I
mentioned Hitler specifically. Adolf turned very red and
asked me to elaborate. When I did, he stormed out of the
room. I didn't see him again until we walked up behind
him in the graveyard."

Max sat down again and leaned back in his chair,
frowning at the ceiling. "I wonder what the hell he
buried?"

Manfred shrugged and answered, "I honestly don't
know. But whatever it was, he took a great deal of care in
hiding it very well, even going so far as to smooth out the
concrete he poured over it. And it must have been very

valuable or very important, because Adolf tried to stab me when he saw us standing there." Running his hands through his hair, Manfred continued, "The only reason the pastor is dead instead of me is because he stepped in front of me at the last minute."

"Sounds to me like the violence was directed at you specifically," Max mused.

Manfred closed his eyes and replayed the scene in his head. "Most definitely," he said, opening them again. "Adolf didn't even look at the pastor, not even when he asked Adolf what he was doing. Adolf was staring at me the whole time."

Max was silent for a bit, then asked, "Do you think he saw you use the tunnel?"

"Possibly," Manfred conceded. "To be honest, once I noticed the light coming toward us, I was only focused on getting into the tunnel and getting that wreath put back into place. At that point I had no idea where Adolf had gone."

"So, we have a former student of yours who sounds like he missed the good old days when Nazis ran the show, burying something that he was willing to kill for under a Wall that for all we know might stand until the end of time. It makes no sense," Max said.

"Well," Manfred pointed out, "the last thing he did before he turned around and saw us was take something out of his pocket – I realize now it was his knife – and make marks on the fresh concrete and on one of the blocks next to it. So maybe he was only putting whatever it was there temporarily, and he means to go get it back later. It would explain the marks – a way to find the location again."

"But the question still remains; why would someone bury something they might not be able to retrieve later? If it's that important, why not just hide it somewhere in their house, like you did with the radio and the gun?" Max wondered aloud.

Then it dawned on Manfred. He leaned forward and said excitedly, "But, if it was anything connected to the Nazis, it would actually be smart to hide it somewhere *other* than in your possession. Right before I left, there were special squads that were being sent randomly to check people's houses in the entire Mitte district. In the little store down the street from the house I overheard a Soviet soldier complaining about being assigned to one of the teams, saying that 'this Nazi hunting is tiresome, surely we have caught them all by now.' Luckily, they didn't get to my house before I crossed over, or they would have found the radio and the gun, and I would be in jail in Berlin instead of here with you."

"And Adolf is one of the brightest students I have ever taught – *ever*," Manfred continued, very slowly. Looking up at Max, he said, "If you still have any contacts over there, you might try to find out what he's put in that Wall. I have a feeling that whatever it is, it's big and very, very dangerous if he gets it back."

"I have just the person who can find out for us," Max replied. "But I need to go back to West Berlin."

***

The pigeon took off effortlessly from the West Berlin balcony, soaring and swooping, heading to the east, its flight path imprinted on its memory. Reaching its destination, the bird touched down gracefully on the rooftop, walking along the precipice. Its trainer gently scooped it up, carried it over to its cage, and removed the piece of paper from the tiny canister fastened to the bird's left leg.

The piece of paper was from Max Jones, Snowbird noted with a delighted smile. He needed some information. Snowbird was to try to find markings on the Wall behind the Church, and also attempt to locate one Adolf Werner. *Werner, Adolf Werner...* Snowbird thought. *Why does that name sound familiar?* Frowning, Snowbird mentally set that puzzle aside, took a little piece of paper and a pencil from a pocket, and began to write.

At least one of the questions Snowbird already knew the answer to.

***

Max watched the bird make its approach. With a final flutter of wings, the creature perched onto the balcony. Max very carefully took the pigeon into his hands and removed Snowbird's elegantly handwritten note from the cylinder. He read:

"Church closed. Guards in bell tower.
Give me two days about the other.
You owe me a beer!

Snowbird"

At the last line, Max roared with laughter. Snowbird always ended with that line; it was both an authenticity code and a running joke between them. But it still made him laugh every time.

Max had met Snowbird entirely by accident one day in 1955. The two had become good friends, and when Max asked for help in getting messages in and out of East Berlin, it was Snowbird's idea to use the carrier pigeons. "Sometimes the old ways are the best ways," Snowbird had said with a mischievous grin.

After the Wall had gone up, the good idea became a great idea; it was pretty much the only means of contact left open that did not involve radio transmissions, which could be traced.

Good luck, Snowbird, Max thought. *Hopefully you will find something we can use.*

Snowbird, meanwhile, had figured out why the name Adolf Werner had sounded so familiar. He'd been a student of Snowbird's in primary school, and his family had lived one block over from here.

"Time to see if Adolf is home," Snowbird said, reaching for the walker. Although Snowbird certainly did not need the walker, it was a necessary part of the illusion maintained in the public eye of being old and frail. This façade enabled Snowbird to pretty much come and go without being bothered; combined with pretending to be senile it worked wonders. East German and Soviet policemen tended to waive old loons on their way rather than have to deal with them. Snowbird, even at seventy-two, was as sharp as ever. It was just a bigger advantage to pretend not to be.

Fully in character, Snowbird shuffled slowly along the sidewalk, receiving friendly greetings from just about every person that passed. Snowbird was well known in the Mitte District and had taught most of the folks living there at one time or another, not to mention owning the candy store at the end of the block since retiring from teaching. Reaching the Werner's house, Snowbird shuffled the walker up the steps and rang the bell. No answer.

Reaching for the doorknob revealed that the door was not locked, so Snowbird went in to have a look around. He immediately noticed that, on the floor in the doorway leading to the kitchen, there was a little wallet-sized photograph of two men and a boy, maybe ten years old.

Obviously, this was not the proper place for it; it must have fallen out of a wallet or pocket.

The boy was definitely Adolf – Snowbird had a steel trap of a memory for faces. They were all dressed in hunting gear and posing with a freshly killed wild boar. Turning the photo over, Snowbird read the caption, written in a child's scrawl: *"Me, Father, and Uncle Ernst – October 1943"*. Gazing at the picture again for a long moment, recognition dawned. Snowbird knew who 'Uncle Ernst' was. Max would definitely want to see this picture.

Stuffing the photograph into a pocket, Snowbird made the slow journey back to the apartment rooftop, being stopped several more times along the way by folks wanting to say hello. The picture was rolled up as tightly as possible and stuffed into a cylinder along with a short note. Then Snowbird set the pigeon loose and watched it fly toward West Berlin.

***

"That was fast," Max said. "Snowbird said two days."

"Well, sir," replied the young man sent to interrupt his meeting, "I don't know about that. I was only told a carrier pigeon had arrived with something you were going to want to see."

The young man was right. Max read the note from Snowbird – *Adolf gone, found this, you should know this face* – and looked long and hard at the picture, swearing softly under his breath. 'Uncle Ernst' was in fact Ernst Kaltenbrunner, the highest-ranking SS officer to be captured alive. Max had spent many hours watching the man during the Nuremberg trials. There had been unsubstantiated claims that Hitler had entrusted one or more members of the SS with top-secret documents; no evidence of those documents had ever been found.

Kaltenbrunner had been a favorite of the Fuhrer. If Adolf Werner referred to this man as Uncle, it lent a great deal of credence to Manfred's theory about something of great importance being buried in that damn Wall. Max quickly penned a note to send back to Snowbird. Then they set the bird free to return home.

Snowbird watched the pigeon land, then retrieved and read the note. *"You are <u>absolutely</u> <u>brilliant</u>! Just the info we needed. I may not be in touch for a while, but I'll be back as soon as I can. Max"*.

Josephine Mueller, called Nana by the entire neighborhood and Snowbird by a select few, beamed.

CHAPTER FIVE

The person of interest in Snowbird's fact-finding mission was not only out of town when she came calling, but he was out of the country. As a matter of fact, he was walking up the gangplank onto a British cruise liner bound for South America with papers that proclaimed him to be a Finn named Larsen.

Adolf had discovered to his dismay that the old pathway in Wismar was closed; the individual his father had guided him to was dead. But he was not wired to give up easily. He sat in a corner of the local pub, nursing a beer and racking his brain to come up with the next step that would get him further along on his quest. He happened to overhear the bartender greeting the huge, menacing-looking man who had just entered as 'Captain Larsen'. The light bulb illuminated in Adolf's head.

He had edged himself out of the little booth, and with mug in hand approached the captain and asked permission to join him. Larsen acquiesced with a hard stare and a grunt, pointing to a chair. Adolf saw no point in wasting time. He sat down, ordered another round for the two of them, then leaned forward and quietly said, "I would like to leave with you when your ship sails. What would it cost me?"

The captain gave him another hard and stony stare for a long while. Just when Adolf thought he'd made a huge mistake, Larsen's face broke into a grin, and the man laughed loud and long.

"Direct and to the point," he said, clamping a massive hand on Adolf's shoulder. "I like it!"

Two days later, Adolf found himself aboard the fishing vessel *Sea Siren*, heading for Amsterdam. It was his first time out on the water, and the seasickness was unbearable; at one point he was convinced that dying would be much simpler. He failed to see how anyone could survive such misery. For Larsen, a fourth-generation fisherman, this caused a great deal of amusement. It was not until day four that Adolf began to feel better, but by that time the massive Finn had already labeled him 'maa-alueiden jalat' – 'land legs'.

The seventy-eight-foot boat had to travel almost due north past Skagen, located at the very tip of Denmark, before turning southward again into the North Sea to reach the Netherlands. When Amsterdam came into view Adolf had felt like cheering. He had also promised himself that any other sea voyages would be done on a much, much bigger boat. He shook hands with Larsen and set foot on dry land with profound relief, some three weeks since the bar in Wismar.

A bath and a bed, he had thought to himself, *and then let's get moving again.* He hefted his pack – which now also contained some money and the passport he had stolen from the captain – onto his shoulders and walked away to find a currency exchange.

***

In Manassas, the Amsels and Meyers had settled into a routine. Rose and Emilie delighted over each crate of belongings that arrived from West Germany, making a game of placing everything just so. When they were finished, the old house glowed with warmth and welcome. Klaus invested in woodworking tools and spent quality time in the basement making beautiful carvings to sell at the annual town festival. Manfred adjusted to teaching World Literature at the University of Virginia, and foreign languages at Quantico and Langley.

Max and Manfred had discussed the information Snowbird had uncovered. "There's just no way to tell where Adolf is now," Manfred observed. "He could still be in Berlin, or a thousand miles from Germany by now."

Max sighed; he knew Manfred was right. They could not cast a net when they had no idea where to cast it, and they did not have any agents in the Soviet sector outside Berlin. And with the church graveyard now under permanent surveillance, any chance they might have had to rediscover Adolf's dig site was lost as well. Other than placing Adolf Werner on the Allies' watch list, they had no recourse but to suspend the pursuit for now.

So, Manfred shifted his focus to introducing group after group of new students to the wonders of learning, whether literature or another language. As always, he was a popular professor on all campuses. His Langley and Quantico courses went a step further, reinforcing to those students that pretending not to understand was also infinitely valuable in their future line of work.

"Some of the best intelligence gathered is done so by just listening to your environment," he stressed to his class. "The key is that you *must* keep a neutral expression, no matter what you've just heard. If your targets even suspect that you understand what is being said, the least that can happen is that they move away where you can no longer overhear them. The worst that can happen is, well, I'm sure you all have very vivid imaginations."

A few of the students nodded solemnly.

***

Adolf stood, stretched, rubbed his eyes, and decided fresh air would do him some good. He had consumed too many cigarettes lately. He poured himself a drink from one of the crystal decanters, then strolled over to the balcony doors and stepped out toward a magnificent view. Swirling the fiery liquid around in his glass, he leaned lazily against the railing, watching the gardeners working in the flowerbeds along the south side of the expansive lawn. Sometimes he still found it hard to believe he had come so far.

The cruise ship Adolf had boarded in Amsterdam in the fall of 1962 had made a day stop in Sao Luis before continuing on to Rio de Janeiro. This was unexpected but benefited his plans greatly. He went ashore with a huge group of other passengers that morning and managed to lift the wallet off an oblivious fellow tourist. When the group returned to the boat at five p.m., they were one short. At nine p.m. the boat's staff, having done a roll call several times, duly notified the port authorities that a Mr. Larsen had failed to return from the shore excursion. By then, Adolf was resting comfortably in a little room under his own name, making plans to head up the coast on the scooter he paid for with stolen cash. Mr. Larsen had ceased to exist for the time being.

The next morning, Adolf went to outfit his traveling kit with clothing more suited to a tropical climate. He picked up two more lightweight long-sleeve button-up shirts, two cotton t-shirts, two pairs of cargo pants, a rain jacket, extra socks, a straw hat, and a second hiking pack.

Returning to his room, he situated his belongings and some foodstuffs into his backpacks and sat on the side of the bed for a moment.

Get to Macapá, Brazil, however you can, his father's letter had read. *Seek out Hans Metzger; he served with me and will guide you further.*

Adolf consulted his map of the region. From Sao Luis to Macapá was a little over 1,000 miles. He folded the map and tucked it into the top of one of the backpacks, looked once around the room to ensure he had everything he needed, then gathered up his packs and went out to the waiting scooter. He placed the larger of the two packs in the basket on the back, strapping it down securely, and hoisted the other onto his shoulders. Mounting the scooter, Adolf set off on the next leg of his journey.

He took his time, only riding about thirty miles a day – the little scooter was not built for marathon runs. He encountered horrible roads but amazing scenery, exquisite food, and friendly locals along the way. It had been the week before New Year's when he had finally arrived in Macapá, and none too soon. The rainy season had begun.

To his amazement, he found that after all these years Herr Metzger was right where Adolf's father had said he would be, in a little cantina on the outskirts of the town. But Metzger had been busy in the eighteen years he had called Brazil home; he now also owned one of the largest mining operations in the region.

Metzger was extremely suspicious of the newcomer at first; being wary was an old, instinctive habit that had kept the ex-SS man alive all these years. But once he realized who Adolf's father had been, he relaxed and welcomed the young man warmly.

"I keep the cantina for fun," he explained to Adolf. "But the real money around here is in exports. In this region it is gold and manganese that lines a man's pockets."

"Your father was a great man, Adolf," he continued. "I had hoped he would make it out. But fate intervened, I suppose. Now, you are here. And because of your father, I will help you in any way I can."

Adolf leaned forward and replied very softly, "I *will* rebuild the Reich, make no mistake about that. How many are left?"

Metzger shook his head. "You and I are the only ones I'm aware of. I have heard of a few others that may have made it out of Germany, but I have never been able to confirm this. As you can imagine, one does not announce affiliations as openly these days."

Adolf thought for a moment, and said, "If it's just us, so be it. We can slowly build strength over time." He proceeded to tell Metzger about the documents he had found in the trunk, and the events that had led him to Macapá.

Metzger's eyes grew wide and bright, but he remained silent until Adolf had finished with "One day, we will return to the Fatherland and reclaim the manifesto."

Metzger raised his glass, and they toasted.

And so, Metzger had taken Adolf under his wing, teaching him everything he needed to know about mining and the export business. Adolf watched and listened, making suggestions here and there that resulted in a huge profit increase in the operations. It quickly became apparent to Metzger that Adolf had a natural head for business, an uncanny ability for management and finances as well as being a sharp judge of character. He instinctively knew when to tread lightly and when to take a hardline approach.

Over time, Metzger began to regard Adolf as the son he never had. So he taught him other things that were equally as important – weaponry, interrogation tactics, and hand-to-hand combat among them. He also insisted that Adolf learn English and Portuguese, which he did with amazing rapidity.

When the old man died in 1982, Adolf inherited the entire empire Metzger had built. He promptly made some deals that netted him a monopoly of the entire gold-exporting business in the northern half of Brazil. More importantly, he continued to cultivate business contacts around the world, including several high-volume gold buyers in the United States and Europe. No more scurrying around with false names under false pretenses. He now had legitimate means to travel anywhere he pleased. The first pieces of the plan had fallen into place beautifully.

The following summer, Adolf had the place built on Lake Manacapuru just outside Manaus, where he now stood on the second-floor balcony and watched a mild afternoon sky beginning to descend into a gorgeous sunset over the Amazon.

***

It must skip a generation in our family, Manfred thought. His father had been a human calculator, figuring complex math problems all in his head as easily as most people breathed. Manfred himself had had to work extremely hard in his math classes to keep his 'A' average through school; his natural talents ran to the right-brain, or artistic side. Yet his son Daniel, from his very first day in kindergarten, was most definitely a left-brain dominant individual just like Manfred's father had been.

Daniel was so gifted that the summer of his sophomore year he decided to take the SAT purely for fun and got perfect scores on all sections. The result was a full scholarship to the College of William and Mary at the age of seventeen for his bachelor's degree. He majored in both Math and Chemistry and graduated at the head of his class just after his twentieth birthday. Daniel then attended the University of Virginia, achieving his Masters' degree in math by the time he turned twenty-two. Next came an invitation to pursue his doctorate at MIT, all expenses paid, in addition to the offer of a teaching position there.

Now Manfred was in a hotel room in Cambridge, Massachusetts, adjusting his new tie, preparing to go and watch his only child graduate with a doctorate at the age of twenty-five.

Where did the time go? he thought to himself as he checked his appearance in the mirror. *It seems like yesterday I was able to hold him in my arms while he slept*. Turning his head to the side slightly, he grimaced as he noticed more and more silver streaks in his hair.

"Darling, you look wonderful – except for the frown," came a voice from the doorway.

He looked over his shoulder, and the frown melted away. After over thirty years together, he still felt that thunderbolt every single time he looked at her. Rose was as stunning as ever. She too had thin, silver ribbons beginning to intertwine with her dark locks. But that was the only way the years had touched her at all.

She smiled and took Manfred's hand in hers. "Shall we go? We don't want to keep Daniel and Hope waiting."

Daniel had met Hope in the summer of 1984 at the University of Virginia. She had been on her way up the steps in front of the library; he had been coming down. When she twisted her ankle and dropped her books and papers, Daniel had been the first to come to her aid, and they had been dating ever since. A history major, Hope was small and delicate, with fiery green eyes and hair the color of warm honey. She had a sparkling laugh and a vivacious personality, and Daniel was in love with her the moment he saw her on the stairs.

Hope had no family to speak of; she too was an only child. Her father had been killed in an industrial accident when she was three, and her mother had lost a battle with cancer in 1982, just before Hope turned twenty. So Daniel had invited her to stay with his family at Christmas that first year. Manfred and Rose had taken to her immediately, and secretly hoped she would become a daughter-in-law at some point.

Now Manfred and Rose sat and visited with Hope, waiting for the commencement ceremony to start. The crowd quieted as the music began and the candidates filed into their seats. They spotted Daniel, tall, broad shouldered, extremely handsome in his robes. He smiled and waved to the three of them, and they smiled and waved back. Both Hope and Rose were already misty-eyed. As Daniel took his seat among his classmates, he surreptitiously reached under his robe to touch the object inside the jacket pocket of his suit. None of them suspected a thing. It was going to be a great day.

***

Adolf's reverie was broken by shouts off to the right. He noticed two of his guards approaching the house with a third person between them.

Frowning, he turned and left the balcony, heading downstairs. He opened the back door and stepped out onto the patio as the guards were escorting their captive up the steps. Adolf froze and stared at the new arrival with undisguised shock. Staring back at him defiantly was a boy, no more than seven or eight at the most. Behind the dirt smudges on his face Adolf noticed a pale complexion with a sprinkling of freckles. But what had him mesmerized was the child's blond hair, almost white, and slate-gray eyes.

"Mr. Werner, we found him sneaking onto the property," one of the guards began. Adolf was studying

the child from his dream so intently that the guard
started to repeat himself, thinking he had not been heard.
He was waved off dismissively.

"Leave us," Adolf barked. "I will take it from here."

Confused, the guards withdrew to continue their
rounds.

"And you," Adolf said to the boy, "Come with me." He
received an icy stare in response, but the boy followed
him inside as directed. Adolf gestured to a chair in the
living area, which the child sat in sulkily.

"And just what do you think you're doing trespassing
on my property?" Adolf asked, taking the opposite chair.
No response. He tried another tack. "You know, I happen
to be friendly with the police chief in Manaus. One phone
call will get you back to your family."

To which the boy bitterly replied, in perfect English,
"I have no family. I ran away from the orphanage. They
didn't want me anyway. They all made fun of me and
called me 'o diabo loiro'. I was just looking for food. I
wasn't going to *steal* anything. Can I go now?"

Adolf had to suppress a grin. "Where would you go?"
he responded.

The boy shrugged his shoulders, then jutted out his
chin and stated, "I'll think of somewhere. I don't need
anybody."

Now Adolf could not help but laugh at this show of
bravado. "O diabo loiro," he repeated. "The blond devil. I
bet you're a handful, aren't you? What's your name?"

"Mikel," the child replied. "And I can take care of
myself."

"I have no doubt of that," Adolf said, not unkindly.
"But how about you stay here and have dinner, Mikel?
Manaus is a long way from here on foot. You must be
tired and hungry."

Those unreadable eyes watched Adolf for a long while
before Mikel responded with a slightly thawed, "Okay."

Over dinner Mikel continued to watch everything
around him, particularly Adolf, with suspicion and

wariness. When the plates were served, the child descended on his food like he'd not eaten in a year. Adolf sat and watched his small charge and remembered the dream he'd had so long ago. This child was meant to find him. He was meant to find this child. One piece of his dream had come to fruition. Adolf had no doubt whatsoever that the rest of it would materialize as well.

Finally, the boy had eaten his fill and was already beginning to show signs of the sleepiness that comes immediately after a contented stomach.

"Mikel," Adolf said softly. "It's dark now. Too late to be traveling. How about you stay here? If you like you can continue your journey in the morning."

Mikel nodded drowsily.

Raisa, Adolf's housekeeper, helped the child up the stairs and showed him to a guest room. She came down five minutes later and approached Adolf, who had moved to the study for a glass of brandy.

"Senhor Adolf, that child fell asleep as soon as he hit the pillow – I barely got his shoes off," she said.

"Thank you, Raisa," he responded. "Would you be so kind as to check on him during the night? And let me know when he wakes."

"Absolutely, Senhor Adolf. Good night." Raisa left the study.

Adolf swirled his brandy and stared into the fire, thinking, remembering.

***

The ceremony had ended, and all the graduates were surrounded by family and friends. Daniel made his way through the throng of people and finally spotted his parents and Hope standing off to one side of the auditorium. He hugged Manfred and Rose, and then Hope threw her arms around him and said, "We are all so proud of you!"

Daniel, smiling mischievously over Hope's shoulder at his mother, replied, "Well, it's just about been the perfect day – almost."

Hope released him and stepped back, slightly confused. Winking at his father, Daniel reached under his robe. Pulling the tiny box from his jacket pocket, he got down on one knee, opened the box, and said to Hope, "Will you marry me?"

***

Adolf came down the stairs to a hearty breakfast, as usual. Raisa believed in starting the morning off right. At the table sat his diminutive houseguest, feet swinging idly underneath his chair, tackling a mountain of pancakes. Adolf poured himself a first cup of Raisa's special coffee blend and took a seat next to Mikel.

"And how did you sleep?" Adolf inquired.

"Pretty good," responded Mikel, around a mouthful of syrupy goodness.

"I happen to have business to attend to in town today. I know you probably want to get going on your way, but I had rather hoped you'd be able to come with me," Adolf mentioned casually.

Mikel paused, fork in midair, and regarded Adolf warily for a moment; then shrugged his shoulders and replied, "Um, sure, if you want," before shoveling another huge bite of pancakes.

"Very well then," said Adolf. "You finish your breakfast and we'll go."

Ten minutes later, they were in the car heading north to Manaus. Adolf's driver, Enrique, navigated as smoothly as ever on the uneven roads into the town. When they pulled up in front of the orphanage, Mikel yelled, "Hey, you tricked me. I don't wanna go back!"

"I did no such thing, Mikel," Adolf stated evenly. "I told you I had business in town today, and I do. Wait here with Enrique. I won't be long." With that, Adolf exited the car and went inside.

Glancing in the rearview mirror, Enrique could see the boy's wheels turning about whether or not to make a run for it. He turned around to look at Mikel. "Hey," he said.

"What?" grumbled the boy.

"Mister Adolf is nice," Enrique said. "You can trust him." The only response he received was an icy stare. But the boy stopped fidgeting and took his hand off the door handle.

About ten minutes later, Adolf returned. "Enrique, head to the marketplace please," he directed. Then he looked at Mikel. "I think you could do with some new clothes. What do you think?" Again, he saw no readable expression in the gray eyes.

There was silence in the car for what seemed like forever. Then Adolf heard a small, muffled sound. He turned his attention from the window and glanced down at Mikel. The child had two tears slowly tracking down his face. "Why are you being nice to me?" Mikel managed.

"Because," Adolf said, "I wasn't too much older than you are when I lost my father. I know how it feels to be disconnected, and think you have to take on the world all by yourself. So," he continued, now with Mikel's undivided attention, "I talked to the headmaster at the orphanage and asked them to send me whatever papers I need to sign to have you come live with me – if you want to, that is."

A spark in those gray eyes and the wisp of a smile was the answer.

CHAPTER SIX

It was two minutes past eight p.m. on November the eighth, 1989, almost twelve hours into the vigil, and Manfred honestly thought Daniel would wear a hole in the floor. Back and forth, back and forth, sitting down for a moment, then up again. Manfred chuckled.
"What's so funny?" Daniel asked.

"Oh, son, you just remind me of me when you were born," Manfred replied. "I paced, I chain-smoked, I drove the nurses crazy with questions every few minutes. Doesn't seem that long ago, either. Now I'm sitting here watching you about to be a father."

Daniel sat beside his father, grabbed the remote for the waiting room television, and began idly flipping channels almost as a reflex action. "I still feel silly for not being able to stay in there," he admitted. "But once I saw the needles, I had to leave."

"In my day, the fathers weren't even invited," Manfred told him. "We were banished to the waiting room. You tried, that's the main thing. And this baby will come regardless of who is and isn't in there."

"Is he as nervous as he looks?" boomed a familiar voice.

Daniel and Manfred turned toward the door and smiled.

"Uncle Max," Daniel said, leaping out of his chair to shake his hand. "It's so good to see you."

"I didn't miss it, did I? Are we still in a holding pattern?" Max Jones shrugged off his overcoat and sat down next to the expectant father.

"Nope, still waiting," Daniel confirmed. "Mom's in there with Hope now."

The three settled into a comfortable silence while Daniel continued to turn the channels. Suddenly Max said, "Stop."

Then Manfred urged, "Turn this up, son."

It was a breaking news story, and the church being shown onscreen was all too familiar.

The volume was increased just in time to hear the reporter say, "This beautiful structure, the Church of Reconciliation on Bernaur Strasse, was made inaccessible to most of its parishioners when the Wall dividing East and West Berlin was built back in 1961. With today's surprise announcement from the East German government, it seems to be only a matter of time before both East and West Berliners will be able to gather here once more."

Max and Manfred looked at each other, absolutely dumbfounded. Daniel said, "Dad. Isn't that the church you told me about? The one you and Mom got married in?"

"Yes, it is," Manfred responded.

"Manfred, when we get things done here, we'll need to…" Max began.

"It looks like we may be taking a trip, Max," Manfred finished.

Just then, one of the obstetric nurses came to the waiting room to find Daniel. "The baby is here and healthy," she said. "And Hope's doing fine, too. Would you like to see them?" Daniel almost ran her over on his way down the hall to his wife and new child.

Manfred and Max took a more leisurely stroll in that direction. "I believe I will wait here," Max said at the doorway. "Take your time."

When Manfred entered the room, Daniel was seated in a chair right next to Hope's bed, cradling an infant in his arms and crying. "It's a girl, Dad, and she's gorgeous," he managed through the tears.

Manfred kissed Hope lightly on the forehead, then walked over to Rose and slipped his arm around her waist. Together, they looked down at their granddaughter.

Hope, tired but smiling, reached out to take Rose's hand and said, "I'm so glad you were here with me. And I know my mom is here in spirit. Daniel and I decided that if we had a girl we would name her Isabella Rose, after her grandmothers." Rose smiled, and gently squeezed her daughter-in-law's hand.

After about half an hour it was obvious that Hope could use some rest. Manfred and Rose kissed and hugged her and Daniel, held Isabella for a few minutes, then stepped out into the hall to give the little family some bonding time. Max was where Manfred had left him, leaning against the wall and looking at his pager.

The men and Rose retreated to the waiting room, where Manfred brought her up to date about the breaking news coming from Berlin while Max made a call. "Oh," she said, her eyes widening. "I guess this means the two of you will be traveling?"

"That's the plan," Max responded, hanging up the phone. "We're on the afternoon flight out from Dulles tomorrow."

***

"...surprise announcement from the East German government, it seems to be only a matter of time before both East and West Berliners will be able to gather here once more."

Adolf turned off the television and sat for a moment, completely stunned. The Wall was going to come down. He had almost given up hope of ever being able to retrieve his treasure; that damn Wall had been in place for... what? Almost thirty years now?

"Mikel," he called, still reeling.

Mikel came in from the library. "Yes, Dad?" he squeaked – his voice was beginning to change, Adolf noted with a touch of amusement.

"Son, something has come up and I need to take a trip. I shouldn't be gone longer than a week, ten days at the most. Be good for Raisa, okay?"

"Okay, Dad." Mikel went back to his books.

Adolf paused for a moment to collect his thoughts, then picked up the phone and dialed. "Hello," he said. "I need a ticket to Germany."

***

The following evening, Adolf was walking through the Hannover airport on his way to baggage claim. He had arranged for a rental car to travel the two hours into Berlin. As he got behind the wheel, he mentally braced himself for the task at hand. Just because the old Church grounds would be accessible, it didn't mean he could be careless. His plan was to find a hotel within reasonable walking distance of the graveyard and make his retrieval under cover of darkness. If all went well, he could be back in Manaus by Monday. Getting his bearings, Adolf left the airport, heading east on A2.

The travel by car went uneventfully. Adolf found himself in awe of how much Berlin had changed in the twenty-seven years he'd been gone. As he made his way further into the heart of the West, half of the city he could see where portions of the Wall had already been removed. The atmosphere around him was euphoric. Gripping the wheel a bit tighter, he maneuvered as close as he dared to his target area.

He spied a hotel ahead on his right and pulled smoothly into the valet parking line. By his estimation, the Church was ahead and to the right approximately five blocks from the hotel.

This could work nicely, he thought, handing his keys to the young man assigned to park his car. He checked in with the reception desk under the name Larsen – no point in taking chances – and settled into the tenth-floor room with an eastward-facing balcony he'd requested. From this vantage point he could easily spot the Church spires and bell tower in the moonlight, just about where he thought they would be. He raised his glass to his empty room and said, "Our triumph is about to begin."

He had to fight the urge to race over and retrieve his prize tonight. *Patience,* Adolf told himself. *You need to do reconnaissance in the daylight first to make sure.* He knew his inner voice was right, but it was still irritating. *Relax. It's been twenty-seven years. One more night won't hurt. Get some sleep.*

Although Adolf did not know it, he was in a race to retrieve the items he had hidden so long ago. Manfred and Max were somewhere over the Atlantic and were scheduled to arrive in London in the wee hours of the following morning. They would be flying in a military transport late in the afternoon that would arrive directly at Templehof around dusk.

***

As Adolf was reluctantly drifting off, Max and Manfred were about forty minutes away from touching down in Glasgow. From there they would hop a smaller aircraft into Heathrow. The two sat in silence for much of the flight, each lost in thought. Manfred's mind had traveled back to the day he and his family had left their homeland. It was amazing to him that almost thirty years had passed since that first white-knuckle flight out of West Berlin.

But we made the right choice, all of us, he thought. Their lives had been fairly quiet since moving to Manassas – at least until yesterday. He smiled. His new granddaughter was just beautiful. Klaus and Emilie would have agreed, had they been there. Emilie had passed in her sleep in 1982, and Klaus followed her about six months later due to a broken heart. *It's the way things go, one big circle,* he mused.

With an effort, he pulled himself out of the past and back to the present. "What's the latest intel from Berlin?" he asked Max.

"Preliminary indications are that pieces of the Wall are already starting to come down toward the edges of the city." Max responded. "Given that your Church is in the heart of it, we may not be able to access it for a while."

"Possibly," Manfred pointed out. "But we should be able to cross at Charlie and at least go take a look, don't you think?"

"We'll see what happens," Max replied.

The announcement to fasten seat belts and secure table trays for the landing interrupted their conversation. Fifteen minutes later, after some of the worst turbulence either had experienced, they were safely on the ground. Disembarking, they headed toward baggage carousel nine, where they were met by RAF Corporal Jennings. Michael Smythe had sent him to collect Max and Manfred.

"Flights in and out of London have been cancelled since this afternoon, sirs," he explained. "It's the fog. Yours is the last flight to land here, right before the heavy stuff rolled in. They've just cancelled remaining flights here, too. We'll have to travel to London by train; the next one leaves in the morning."

"What about being able to leave London?" Max asked.

"Sir, the best reports indicate the weather should clear sometime tomorrow afternoon," Jennings replied.

"Well, that screws up our plans a bit," Max muttered. He turned to Manfred and said, "How about dinner? We seem to have some time on our hands."

***

Adolf woke with the breaking dawn, slowly, leisurely. Stretching, he flipped the covers back and strode to the window to watch the dark sky transform into brilliant pinks and oranges. It was his first sunrise in his homeland in a very long time. He had been gone half his life.

He ordered eggs, sausages, toast, and coffee from room service at six. Then, whistling a little tune, he walked into the bathroom for a quick shower. He was dressed and tying his shoes when the food arrived. Adolf gestured to the balcony, and the server maneuvered the trolley to the door and placed the breakfast tray on the patio table. Adolf tipped him, saw him out, then sat down to his meal.

The first bite into one of the sausages almost drove him to tears – he had forgotten how exquisite German sausages were. Funny that he'd taken them for granted back when he could get them all the time. Savoring each morsel, he sat contentedly on his balcony and watched Berlin come awake.

***

Max was more right about time than he knew. The corporal's news had been too optimistic. Fog held the region in its grip for over twenty hours and counting. In Smythe's office in London, Max and Manfred were dealing with boredom and anticipation. The train had delivered them into London around noon, the same time the transport into West Germany had been scheduled to take off. Since then, they'd been waiting on a call hoping to receive takeoff clearance. But the weather had failed to cooperate so far.

The phone rang shrilly just after five pm. Michael picked it up with an abrupt "Yes?" He listened, then smiled and said, "Very well." He replaced the receiver and gestured to the two anxious men sitting in his guest chairs.

"Seems you gents have caught a break," he said. "You need to get yourselves up to the RAF base in Greenham, about an hour north of here. They're saying you should be able to fly out between eight and nine tonight if the weather comes clear like they expect it to." Glancing at his watch, he continued, "You'll need to leave here in the next half hour at the latest. London traffic is ghastly in the evenings."

***

A pretty good day, Adolf reflected, as he sat down to a sumptuous meal of mushroom rouladen and broad noodles. Crossing over into East Berlin had been childishly simple, almost anticlimactic given that the last time he was in Berlin he was heading out of town and was almost caught and shot. As he strolled down the sidewalk, he passed an extremely old woman shuffling with a walker. A flicker of familiarity ran through his memory and was just as easily gone. Adolf continued toward the Church, paying no mind to her.

He'd been pleasantly surprised to see that not only had his treasure remained undiscovered, but that markings he had made on the bricks so long ago were still visible if one knew where to look. He also noted that, about ten feet away, there was now a huge piece of concrete where once a tunnel opening had been. *Guess the Stasi found the tunnel,* he thought absently. All he had to do now was wait for nightfall, and he could unearth his package and be on his way.

As he chewed another bite of rouladen, he reviewed his plan again to make sure there were no flaws. He'd already purchased a few tools and stashed them in the little shed at the back of the church. He had no real concerns about anyone connected with the Church discovering him – it had evidently been closed for years.

He glanced at his wristwatch – a little over an hour before sunset, he guessed. He smiled a strange little smile, took another sip of beer, and continued his delicious dinner.

***

Snowbird could not possibly get home fast enough. *Damn these arthritic knees,* she thought. These days she really did need the walker. But her mind was as sharp at ninety-seven as it had ever been. She had recognized Adolf the moment he went past her. *I have to tell Max,* she told herself, *or at least somebody in the West who can tell him*. After what seemed an eternity, she was finally on her rooftop with her beloved birds. She chose her favorite, fastened the note to its leg, and set it loose.

***

Max and Manfred touched down at Tempelhof around nine-thirty p.m. Their plane was immediately met by a jeep and driver, who said, "Mr. Jones, we have a message for you that arrived via pigeon this afternoon. It was marked urgent."

Max took the note, read it, and cursed aloud. "Manfred, look," he muttered, thrusting the note out.

Manfred reached for it with a growing dread. *I saw Adolf Werner this afternoon*, it said.

"Max," Manfred stated solemnly, "we need to get to the Church."

They climbed into the Army jeep and drove as fast as they dared. They were waved through Checkpoint Charlie almost as if the city had never been divided. The driver stopped in front of the church and had not even shifted into park when Max and Manfred leapt from the vehicle and started around the side of the building, flashlights on.

"Where is it?" Max urged.

"Give me a moment. I have to get my bearings," Manfred said. He oriented himself by glancing at the church, then said, "This way, follow me." They traveled to the southernmost edge of the graveyard and saw what used to be the tunnel opening, now sealed with concrete.

"Maybe that's why Peter tried going over rather than under," Manfred muttered bitterly. Pointing to his right, he continued, "The area Adolf was digging in is over there, about ten feet away. We'll have to look for some markings."

"Dammit, dammit, dammit," Max said. "No, we won't. Look."

They trained their lights and stared despondently at the freshly dug empty hole at the base of the Wall.

***

"And how many bags will you be checking this evening, sir?" the overly perky booking agent at Hannover airport asked.

"Just one," the passenger said, hefting his suitcase onto the scale.

"Very well," she replied briskly.

"Oh, and miss? I would like to upgrade to first class, please," he said.

After a few more keystrokes he was on his way to his terminal gate, boarding pass in his left hand, the keys to his kingdom tucked securely in the briefcase in his right.

He boarded and took his seat on the aisle, placing his briefcase next to him against the bulkhead. A flight attendant asked him if he preferred a mixed drink or champagne.

"Champagne, I think – it's been a very good day," Adolf said with a smile.

SECTION THREE: - Full Circle –

1997 - 2009

CHAPTER SEVEN

"Coming," Manfred called out as he traveled from the living room to answer the front door. He stopped, stooping down, and said in a loud, gruff voice, "Who comes knocking at my door?"

The giggle of delight that sounded from the other side gave him his answer. He swung open the door and was immediately rushed for a hug and kiss by his granddaughter. Picking her up, he twirled her around. "Hello, my Bellissima," he said.

"Hi, Grandpa," Bella said. "Guess what? I got all A's on my report cards all year, and I got the third-grade citizenship award, and we went for ice cream, and..."

"Bella, for goodness' sake," Hope said, laughing. "You've got a whole week to spend with Grandma and Grandpa. There'll be plenty of time to tell them everything that's happened since Easter."

The child's pout was short-lived when she spied Rose in the kitchen doorway.

"I sure wish someone was willing to taste the cookies for me to make sure they're all right," Rose offered. Daniel and Bella's faces both lit up, and everyone laughed as they headed toward freshly baked chocolate chip cookies.

"So, does it feel like ten years have passed already?" Rose asked Hope.

"Yes and no," Hope said. "Daniel and I are so in sync that sometimes it's like we've been married fifty years instead of just ten. Other times I look at him and he still takes my breath away, like when we were dating."

Rose responded with a knowing smile.

Daniel, meanwhile, handed his dad a slip of paper. "This is where we'll be staying in Kentucky, if you need to reach us."

"Nonsense," Manfred replied. "We'll be fine here. Go focus on your lovely bride. A ten-year anniversary is a special thing, a milestone. Go enjoy it, and we'll see you when you get back."

Manfred, Rose, and Bella stood on the front porch and waved until Daniel and Hope were out of sight. Then Manfred looked down and said, "Who's up for popcorn and a movie?"

Seeing a raised eyebrow from Rose, he added, "After dinner, that is."

***

Hope reached over and took her husband's hand as they talked and drove east. They had booked a week at a bed and breakfast nestled in the Appalachian Mountains, and they had both been looking forward to the trip.

He's my best friend, she thought as she listened to him talking. *God, we are so lucky. So many couples never find what we have.*

"Baby, I have a surprise for you," Daniel was saying. "I found out they've got a fair going on this weekend in Charleston. So, I booked a room there for tonight, and we'll get to the B&B on Sunday. Wanna ride the Ferris wheel with me?"

"Only if you buy me cotton candy." She smiled and squeezed his hand.

Later, as they sat snuggled in a cart at the top of the Ferris wheel watching the sunset, Hope laid her head on Daniel's shoulder and sighed contentedly. "Honey," she said, "thank you so much for this. It's just beautiful."

Daniel pulled her closer, kissing her forehead, and replied, "Yep, just about been the perfect day."

Hope raised her head. She had planned on telling him while they were in the mountains, but she couldn't wait.

"How attached are you to the home office?" she asked.

He raised an eyebrow and said teasingly, "I have you up here in a romantic setting, watching a beautiful sunset, and that's what's on your mind? The home office?"

"No, seriously, I need to know," she replied. "Unless you can think of another room in our house that will make a good nursery."

The beautiful sunset they had been watching paled in comparison to the love and joy that spread across his face. "Really?" he asked.

"Really," she said. "The doctor called me this morning. I'm due around Christmas."

***

Rose and Manfred sat watching the fireflies in the backyard. Bella was safely tucked into bed upstairs; she had fallen asleep just after the Beast had turned back into the Prince. Although she had seen the movie hundreds of times, it never got old. And they never tired of watching her joy.

The phone ringing broke the comfortable silence. Manfred returned a few minutes later with a smile on his face. "That was Daniel and Hope, checking in on Bella," he said, chuckling. "They're in Charleston at a county fair. I told them whatever you do, don't tell Bella you had rides and cotton candy without her."

***

Daniel replaced the phone on the hook and stepped out of the phone booth. "She's sleeping already," he told his wife.

"I could have told you that," Hope replied. "And I bet *Beauty & the Beast* is what sent her off to sleep, too."

"Oh yes," Daniel responded. "Dad made sure he mentioned the movie. How many times has she watched it? A hundred? Two hundred?"

"I actually think it's even higher than that," Hope said as they climbed into the car. "But it's at least got a good moral-of-the-story thing going on."

"Well, I think we ought to find some ice cream and celebrate our other thing going on," Daniel said, leaning over to kiss her. "We passed a little parlor when we came into town. Let's head there."

"Sounds good. The baby's been craving mint chocolate chip," Hope replied with a mischievous smile.

They maneuvered out of the dusty parking lot and headed toward dessert. As Daniel drove, he could not keep from smiling. The love of his life was carrying his second child. He had wanted to tell his dad on the phone, but Hope had made him promise to wait until they came back from their trip. She wanted to tell them, and Bella, in person.

***

Stan just didn't feel right. He had been driving the same route now for twenty-five years, and it had never exhausted him like it did today. *Damn this getting old stuff,* he thought. He had just turned fifty. But his doctor said the same thing every year at the physical – *Stan, you're healthier than some twenty-year-olds I've seen.*

But today he'd just been really tired. Fortunately, he was almost back to the yard, and he could drop the trailer and go home and rest. *Maybe it's the flu or something*, he thought. *I just wish this God-awful headache would go away.* Luckily, he was off for the next two days. That would give him a chance to kick whatever bug had him feeling like hell.

As he made his way down Main, he noticed a little passenger car ahead of him waiting at the light. Suddenly, his vision seemed to explode into a multi-color starburst. His head felt like it was splitting in two at the right temple. His last conscious thought was of a stabbing ache behind his right eye. Then there was only darkness as he slumped forward.

***

Daniel happened to glance up. He froze, looking in his rear-view mirror in shock.

"Honey, hang on," he shouted to Hope. "The truck's not stopping!"

He started to try turning the car hard to the left.

But he was too late.

Thirty-five thousand pounds of accelerating big rig tore into the helpless little car at just over fifty miles an hour with a horrific thud. The car followed the direction its front wheels were pointed and snapped around, heading underneath the side of the truck's trailer just behind the cab. Amidst the shrieks of steel impacting steel and booms of blowing tires a single scream sounded, followed by an eerie silence.

An eternity of seconds passed before each vehicle came to rest almost one-hundred feet from the point of impact, with the trailer's back wheels lodged firmly on top of the car. Onlookers rushed to help and were driven back as the car's ruptured fuel tank exploded into flames.

***

Manfred and Rose's front door chime sounded around two a.m. *This had damn well better be important,* Manfred thought as he groggily pulled on his robe and staggered to the front door. He opened it, blinking in disbelief. What the hell were two policemen doing on his front porch at this time of morning?

"Manfred Amsel?" the younger officer asked.

"Yes," Manfred said, rather curtly.

"Sir, we need to talk to you and your wife. May we come in please?" the older of the two asked.

"Certainly," Manfred replied with a knot of fear growing in his belly. "Have a seat in the living room. My wife and I will be down shortly."

The policemen showed themselves to the living area while Manfred went upstairs to wake Rose. The knot in his stomach had tripled in size. He roused her, and hand in hand they returned downstairs.

The older officer pulled his chair beside the couch where Rose and Manfred had sat down nervously. "Sir, Ma'am, my name is Thomas, and I'm the police chaplain," he began gently. "Daniel and Hope were involved in an accident up in Charleston this evening."

***

Bella sat in the window seat with her forehead leaning against the glass, looking out at the rain, the pain in her heart mocked by the spatter against the window panes. Manfred and Rose stood in the doorway, knowing exactly how she felt, unsure how to comfort her.

It had been a little bit easier on them to only have graveside services – open casket had just not been possible. Twin coffins lowered into the earth simultaneously as "Amazing Grace" played solemnly in the background. Then family and friends had retreated to the Amsel home to support one another and to grieve three lives lost – the news of Hope's pregnancy had been relayed by the coroner.

Finally, Rose, Manfred, and Bella were alone. Bella had not cried or said a word in the last three days. While they were extremely concerned about her, Manfred and Rose knew she needed to process what had happened in her own space and in her own way. So they stood, arms around each other, watching, hoping their granddaughter would reach out.

Now she turned to them, tears flowing freely, and said, "I guess this is my home now." Her body racking with sobs, she ran for them blindly.

"Oh, Bellissima," Manfred whispered, scooping her up in his arms. He walked back over to the window seat with her, Rose close behind. Sitting down with Bella, Manfred and Rose both wrapped their arms around her, and their tears mingled with hers.

For a long while they sat huddled together, a ragged band of survivors overwhelmed with grief and pain. No words were spoken; there were none that could make it better.

Eventually, Bella's thin frame shook less and less, and her breathing became less hitched. Manfred very gently picked her up and Rose pulled back the bedcovers. Placing Bella as softly as possible into her bed, Manfred and Rose kissed her on the forehead and quietly left her to sleep.

CHAPTER EIGHT

"You must remember not to give your enemy advance notice of your movements, Mikel," Adolf said, stretching out a hand to help him up off the floor. "The unexpected gives you the advantage in a fight. Try it again."

They repositioned and once again Mikel lunged with the training knife, but this time in a sideswiping motion, forcing Adolf to pivot on the knee he had strained two days ago. "That's it," Adolf remarked, albeit with a wince. "Much better. Always search out your enemy's point of weakness and exploit it. Everyone has one."

Mikel grinned in response.

He has natural ability, and no qualms whatsoever about using it, Adolf thought while smiling back. *I'm glad he's on my side.*

Another thirty minutes, and the session was over. Mikel headed for a run and then a shower. Adolf made his way to the hot tub and sank aching joints gratefully into the warmth.

Flipping on the jets, he reflected on Mikel's training to date. Adolf had passed on all the knowledge he had received from his real and surrogate fathers. He brought in the best tutors money could buy to make sure Mikel had the best possible education. He also baptized Mikel's mind into Nazi beliefs. The boy took to the mantra as naturally as breathing, which pleased Adolf greatly.

And now his adopted son was seventeen, and a good six inches taller than Adolf. He had become a perfect example of Hitler's 'master race' – tall, blond, magnificently built, with those ghostly gray eyes that took in everything and conveyed nothing. Mikel was also completely lethal, with or without a weapon. Most importantly, he had an unswerving loyalty both to Adolf and to the Reich.

Leaning back slightly in the spa, Adolf had a revelation. *That's the way to build my army,* he realized. *Take in troubled kids that no one wants.* It would provide a reputable cover for recruitment. Grinning, he sank a little deeper into the water.

Now his mind turned to the other matter at hand – where to resurrect the Reich. Brazil had been very good for him, no doubt, but was hardly a launching point. *What about America?* he asked himself. *Freedom of everything there. Hell, not even border guards – go where you want, when you want, all across the United States. Play your cards right and no one suspects anything until it's too late.*

He liked it, the dark irony of it. America, one of the cursed enemies that helped destroy his Fuhrer, could now be the birthplace of the Reich coming back to glory. He even knew the perfect place in America – he had foreseen it in his dreams so many years ago. The desert. Arizona. Climbing out of the hot tub, he reached for a towel and headed indoors to make a couple of calls.

***

"This doesn't feel right," Bella Amsel said, frowning. Glancing at her grandparents in the mirror, she continued, "Is the front of this thing supposed to be low like this?"

Manfred chuckled. "I know it seems strange, but yes – the front of the mortarboard cap is supposed to come to about mid-forehead, hit a couple of inches above the eyebrows."

"Well, whoever invented these had no sense of fashion," Bella remarked with a mischievous twinkle. She twirled around in her cap and gown, and with one hand on her hip, said, "How do I look?"

"Stunning as ever," Rose replied. "Just one thing's missing." Stepping forward, she fastened the strand of tiny pearls around Bella's neck. She kissed Bella's cheek, held her hands, and asked, "Are you nervous about your speech?"

"A little," Bella admitted. "I mean, I knew I'd have to give one, being the valedictorian. But it's one thing to practice in your room and another to stand in front of the entire school and do it."

"You'll be fine, Bellissima," Manfred soothed. "You're like a cat – you always land on your feet."

As they headed down to the car, Bella said, "Oh, I was thinking about what we talked about. I do want to start college over the summer term. The sooner I get started, the sooner I can finish."

"I still think you ought to take a little break, sweetheart," Rose answered. "But of course, it's your decision."

Forty-five minutes later, Manfred and Rose were beaming with pride as their granddaughter was among the graduates taking their seats for the ceremony.

Rose grasped her husband's hand, leaned her head on his shoulder, and whispered, "When do you think we ought to tell her, dear?"

"After the ceremony, my love," Manfred replied, clasping her tiny hand with both of his. "Let's tell her tonight."

***

"A pleasure, as always, Mr. Metzger," the Senator said, striding forward with an outstretched hand to greet his guest. "How are things in Macapa?"

"As usual," Adolf remarked. "The mining business continues much as it has been for decades. My reason for coming to see you is of a completely different nature."

"Would you like some coffee?" asked the Senator, motioning Adolf toward an overstuffed armchair.

"That would be nice," Adolf replied, reclining gracefully in his Armani suit.

"I understand you've done quite well with your troubled youth programs in Virginia, Chicago, and Philadelphia," the Senator said, making small talk as the aide brought forward cups.

"Indeed," Adolf responded. "We have several hundred young men whose lives we are helping to turn around." And he thought, *Oh, if you only knew...*

The two watched the aide set the coffee service in silence. Once the young man had departed, Adolf poured himself a cup, added cream and sugar, stirred it delicately, and said, "Senator, I have two propositions for you. The first is that I would like to expand the troubled youth programs to facilities across the country, and I would like to build the headquarters in Phoenix. There are so many more kids out there without families that need guidance. We can reach more of them if we go nationwide."

"Quite a noble undertaking," the Senator murmured.

"The second request is rather... unique. But not only will it bring a very healthy revenue stream into your home state, it will have the environmentalist movements you champion making huge leaps forward, and your colleagues eating out of your hand."

The Senator leaned forward, intrigued. "And what, pray tell, would accomplish that?"

"Water power," Adolf said simply.

"What?" the Senator asked.

"Water power," Adolf repeated. "I have some brilliant men, engineers and scientists, that work for me in Brazil. We are very close to figuring out how to harness heavy water to power machinery. But as you can imagine, the resources to pursue this are more plentiful here in the United States than in South America."

"Impressive, and revolutionary. But what does this have to do with me?" the Senator queried.

"Well," Adolf replied, "I would like to build a facility in your state to pursue this research. If it goes the way I think it will, it will greatly benefit us both, as well as the world."

He stood and walked to the window.

"Think of it, Senator," he continued, gazing out the window, "no more bickering about holes in the ozone, no more wars over out-of-control oil prices. Water is plentiful and recyclable. Many more jobs created here in the United States, and so forth. Everyone wins. And you will be revered for your pivotal part in it all."

Turning from the window, he stated, "But, I need your help to obtain permits and so forth. The sooner this project starts, the better. With any luck, you'll be able to present a brilliant alternative energy bill to the House and Senate within the next four years."

Gazing at the Senator, Adolf rejoiced inside. He could tell the man had fallen for it hook, line, and sinker. But his face remained impassive as he asked, "What do you think? May I count on your assistance, Senator?"

"I see no reason why Metzger Industries wouldn't be able to build a place in Arizona," smiled the Senator. "Let me know what you need. I'll make sure you don't run into any problems. Did you have a specific area in mind?"

***

Manfred, Rose, Bella, and Bella's best friend Stacy sat together around the dinner table, commenting on the ceremony.

"Bel, your speech was so amazing," Stacy said. "Were you nervous? Cause you didn't look nervous at all. Seriously."

"I was absolutely petrified," Bella said with a little laugh. "But I got through it somehow."

"So, Stacy, Bella told me you've been accepted into the University of Phoenix also," Rose commented. "That's wonderful. I suppose the two Musketeers will be roommates?"

"That's the plan, Mrs. A," Stacy replied. "I'm so excited. I know Bel's wanting to get started out there right away, but I'm not planning on going out until the fall semester. I want to have one last summer home with no commitments before I dive into the college world."

"Still planning on studying chemistry, Stacy?" Manfred asked as he scooped up a forkful of cheddar mashed potatoes.

Stacy sipped her tea before saying, "Yes, sir. But I've been thinking about it, and I'm leaning more toward a double major now – chemistry and math."

"Ew," Bella chimed in. "Give me literature or language any day."

At this, everyone laughed.

Stacy and Bella had been best friends since fourth grade, although they were polar opposites – Stacy was short with an athletic build, red hair, green eyes, and freckles and a fiery personality to match, who lived and breathed the sciences. Bella, on the other hand, was tall and slender, ebony hair and cornflower blue eyes, and had a passion for music, literature, and languages. But they had a friendship that transcended the differences.

"Well, I'm pleased our Bellissima will be out in Arizona with at least one person she knows," Manfred stated. "Her grandmother and I will rest a little easier knowing the two of you are together so far from home." Rose nodded in agreement.

Dinner was finished and a bit more small talk was made before Stacy headed home to her aunt's house two blocks over. Manfred and Bella washed and dried the dishes and Rose handled putting everything away.

As the last fork went into the drawer, Manfred looked at his wife, who nodded. "Bella," he said, "come sit down with us for a bit."

They sat at the little table in the breakfast nook, and Manfred and Rose broke the news as gently as they could. "Bella," Rose said. "You know I've not been feeling well lately. "

"I know," Bella said. "I've been concerned about you."

"Well, sweetheart, Dr. Gable had some tests run. Your grandfather and I got the results yesterday afternoon."

"And?" Bella said with a raised eyebrow and a knotted stomach.

"It's cancer, sweetie," Rose said simply.

Immediately Bella's hand shot from her lap to grab her grandmother's. Squeezing Rose's hand, she asked, "So what do we do now?"

"We'll be scheduling surgery sometime in the next few weeks," Manfred answered, covering their hands with his. "Dr. Gable seems to think that we can get it all surgically. Then a round of chemo just to make sure. But the prognosis is good," he added hastily as he watched Bella's eyes swim with tears. "He says we caught it early."

Bella straightened her shoulders, looked Rose in the eyes, and said, "I'm not leaving for Arizona until I know you're okay."

***

Adolf smiled to himself as the limo made its way through the traffic around DuPont Circle.

That was even easier than I thought, he mused.

He knew the Senator was an avid environmentalist but also power-hungry and full of self-importance; he had counted on the man reacting precisely as he did. The whole heavy water thing was a complete ruse, of course. But no one needed to know that except him and Mikel. He had no intention of squandering any more time and money than was necessary to keep the charade in place until his armies were ready to strike.

In the meantime, his capability to recruit young minds into the fold would increase exponentially. *Not much longer, really,* his inner voice said. *I'll have this nation on its knees bowing to Nazi superiority within the next five years at this rate.*

He raised the privacy shield, picked up the car's telephone, and dialed. "Mikel," he murmured, "I'm on the way back. We have much to do."

***

"How are you feeling today, Grandma?" Bella asked as she opened the curtains a bit.

"Much better," Rose replied, sitting up a little. "Looking forward to today being over with."

"Me too," Bella said, coming to sit on the side of the bed. "But you've handled the treatments brilliantly. Just one more, and you're done."

"Thank God for that," Rose answered. "And then, young lady, you can stop fussing over me and get yourself out to Phoenix. The fall term starts in two weeks, and you need to allow time to get settled in out there."

"Are you running me off, Granma?" Bella asked with a mock pout.

Rose laughed. "Not at all, dear. But I'm fine, I promise. Everything has gone better than we hoped so far – right, my love?" she asked as Manfred appeared in the doorway with a tray.

"Absolutely, sweetheart," he answered, moving closer with breakfast. "They were even able to spare that glorious hair of yours." He set the tray across Rose's lap, then leaned forward and kissed her gently.

The three made small talk while Rose ate. And Manfred was right. Dr. Gable had opted for radiation therapy instead of the chemo, and in minimal amounts – the tumor had been completely removed with surgery. Although she had been very tired after each round, Rose still had her lovely dark locks, albeit more tinged with silver than before.

They dressed and gathered their things for the trip to the treatment center. As they walked out to the car, Stacy arrived on her bicycle.

"Good, I made it in time," she said, huffing as she dismounted and walked toward them. "I was running late and worried I would miss you."

"You're welcome to come with us," Rose offered. "But I have to warn you it will be pretty dull for you, waiting around while I get the treatment."

"But it's your last one, and I feel like you're my Granma too, so I really want to come," Stacy said, smiling. "Besides, I brought the school catalog with me. I figure Bel and I can look at some stuff about the campus.

We also need to decide something on room colors," she finished, looking at Bella with a raised eyebrow.

"I thought we settled on pink polka dots," said Bella with mock seriousness.

"Perish the thought – neither of us are that girly!" Stacy said.

"Pink polka dots? Makes my head hurt. All right, you two, in the car," Manfred said with an exaggerated scowl.

All four of them laughed at this. The girls piled into the backseat. Manfred made sure Rose was belted safely into the front seat, then took his place behind the wheel. As they pulled down the driveway, he thought, *thank you, Lord, this is the last time we'll have to make this trip.*

Almost as if she knew what he was thinking, Rose reached over quietly and squeezed his hand, then leaned back against the headrest and smiled as she listened to her granddaughter and her best friend argue prints versus paisley.

***

"Well, what do you think so far?" Adolf asked, gesturing to the drawings.

"Spectacular, Father," Mikel answered, peering slightly over Adolf's shoulder. "What direction will it face?"

"The front gate will be over there," Adolf indicated to his left. "The drive will proceed this way about three-hundred meters. The front steps will be just about twenty feet to our right. Of course, from the ground floor up it will look and function like a boarding school. The subfloors, however, will have state-of-the-art security. No one will get down there unless they are allowed to by us."

"And the rooms?" Mikel inquired.

"Connected by a tunnel from sub-floor three," Adolf responded. "And I think you will be very pleased with the accoutrements I have planned there."

The men turned and walked slowly, studying the blueprint as they went. "What were you thinking about perimeter wall height?" Mikel asked.

Adolf shrugged. "Not sure yet. It has to be a fortress without the appearance of one. People will be suspicious of an exterior wall topped with razor wire around what's supposed to be the headquarters of a youth program."

Mikel walked silently for a moment, then said, "What if we modified the exterior wall so that when the time comes to unveil the Reich, it can have razor wire on top?"

Adolf stopped in his tracks. He turned to his adopted son and said, "What did you have in mind?"

Mikel grinned.

***

"Ladies and gentlemen, if I might have your attention please," the Senator said. "I would like to welcome you all to this ribbon-cutting ceremony. We stand here on the threshold of this magnificent structure, which will give help and hope to so many young men and women in need. I hope that today marks a great chapter in this country's commitment to its young people, the backbone of its future." He paused to receive polite applause.

"I would like to introduce to you the man who has invested so much in the future of America's children," he continued. "Ladies and gentlemen, Mr. Adolf W. Metzger." He gestured Adolf toward the podium.

Adolf waited for the crowd to stop clapping. Then he spoke. "I am honored that you could all join us today," he intoned. "This building, whose doors we're about to open for the first time, marks a continuing commitment to troubled youths all over the United States. This journey began several years ago, with pilot programs in Chicago, Philadelphia, and Virginia. The success of these locations became the catalyst that brings us here today. With expansion of our outreach programs nationwide, we will be able to forever change thousands of young lives."

As he spoke, smoothly delivering the speech he had rehearsed, Adolf's mind was somewhere else. *So close, we are so close,* the voice in his head repeated in sing-song fashion. He felt like dancing, but with practiced self-control returned his full attention to the enraptured crowd before him.

"And so, let me welcome you all to the Metzger Youth Institute," he finished. Moving to the front of the podium, he and the Senator posed with the ribbon and oversized scissors for several flashbulbs before making the ceremonial cut.

Later, as he mingled and made small talk, he noticed the Senator approaching from the left. Gracefully extracting himself from his present conversation, he strolled along with the Senator down the hall and showed the politician into his office.

"I'm impressed, Adolf," the Senator said, shaking Adolf's hand. "This place is absolutely beautiful."

"Thank you, Senator,' Adolf replied silkily. "We already have a hundred and forty-five young people from Oregon and California scheduled to arrive here within the week, and we've have received inquiries from state foster homes in Texas, New Mexico, Utah, and Missouri."

"What's the total capacity here?"

"We planned for up to five hundred as a start," Adolf replied, pouring himself and his guest a drink. "And we allotted space on the grounds for expansion. If we have the success I think we will, we may be adding wings to this building within the next two years."

"By the way," the Senator remarked as he accepted the glass his host offered him, "I spoke to the Chancellor at the University. They are very receptive to your request to build an internship program in conjunction with your Foundation. It would provide their graduates an excellent opportunity to incur some real-life teaching experiences, and you with a steady stream of very intelligent instructors and tutors."

"Most definitely a win-win," Adolf replied. "It will also allow me to perhaps expand the curriculum here." And in his mind, he thought, *and yet another opportunity to build my army.*

"Any problems receiving accreditation?" asked the Senator.

"None." Adolf smiled. "Everything went smoothly."

"So," said the Senator, swirling his drink, "Any progress on the research facility?"

A-hah, Adolf thought. *Finally, we reach the true topic he's interested in.*

"Not as much as there should have been to date," Adolf replied. "My focus has been getting this place up and running first."

The Senator did a poor job of concealing a disappointed look, and said, "Understandable. The kids must come first, of course."

What a crock, Adolf's mind ranted. *This arrogant bastard wants the money and the limelight that 'heavy water' would bring. He's in for such a shock!*

But he simply smiled, laid a hand on the Senator's shoulder, and said, "All in good time. It will be worth the wait, I assure you."

***

Want to know what happened next?

Read <u>Book of Secrets</u> – FREE!

Visit my author site at www.2ofharts.com

Join my newsletter and receive 'Cast of Characters', a supplement to the series, Free!

One of the best things an author can receive is honest feedback about their work.

If you could take just a moment or two and leave a review on my book on Goodreads and other similar places, it would mean the world.

https://www.goodreads.com/author/show/18999540.D_F_Hart

I appreciate your support!

www.ingramcontent.com/pod-product-compliance
Lightning Source LLC
Chambersburg PA
CBHW050154110726
47898CB00008B/2803